BACKTRACK

by

Stewart Seviour

Contents

PREFACE

Although this story is pure fiction, I have drawn on certain real life locations, both in Somerset and in Spain, but with changed place names. Likewise, one or two of the story´s characters are loosely based on people I either knew, or had heard about as a youngster.

In an attempt to weave a fictitious tale out of memories and experiences, readers may identify my sources of inspiration and information. For instance, the Somerset villages, the Benedictine Abbey and School, and the rural railway are all based on fact, as is the restoration of the abandoned S&D station by the Steam Preservation Group.

Of the characters, the old lady who lived alone in a cottage in the woods is based on a real life figure. In fact, I am indebted to her grandson and other local villagers who have freely given information and assurances about her. The father of a schoolfriend did die young due to his suffering as a POW of the Japanese, and I was told at the time that he really did see the supernatural visions I describe. Mild religious tensions did exist in villages during the time I write about, and some clergymen have made an impression on my memory.
Hopefully, I haven´t offended anyone else´s memories!

Parts of Book Two are also based on fact, in particular the rural town in Extremadura, and the controversial plans to build on agricultural land there.

Passages on post war world tensions, the Spanish Civil War, General Franco etc. are also a mixture of research and make believe.

Stewart Seviour
Malaga, Spain
2016

PART ONE – Post-War Britain

In 2010 the British Government released another batch of its secret files, this time ones which spanned the last sixty years, ie: up to 1950. Amongst these files was certain information on a case that involved MI5, one of the government's secret service agencies, and related to a previously little known investigation they undertook in 1948. The main reason for the secrecy surrounding this episode was the potential embarrassment and long term damage the British Government could have suffered should the affair ever have been made public. MI5 matters are rarely discussed anyway of course, but in the immediate post-war years tensions were running high at executive level.

What made the 1948 affair interesting was that it centred around occurrences in a small West Country village, occurrences that were of an international nature, and involved serious crime and treason. Fugitives had fled London carrying damning evidence, and it was MI5's job to apprehend them. This had to be done with as little publicity as possible though, and their agents found themselves working against the clock and coming up against not only danger, but also local and religious tensions in the tight knit, rural community.

What made this particular Somerset village unique, and home to murder and deception? MI5 would discover the link, but that didn't make their job any easier.

Could this threat to Britain still be valid some sixty two years later? Certain cabinet ministers of an EU member state thought so. The affair may have been long ago, to them it had been sleeping, but it could still have relevance to their country now. News of the file's release was soon reported.

The Foreign Minister in question knew that the days of his unpopular government were numbered, but with the country in the midst of a large financial crisis, perhaps some sort of scandal or revelation might help them in the upcoming general elections. After all, they had nothing to lose…

CHAPTER 1

The Spring of 1948 had so far been a good one, at least in the West Country, and the warm weather of late April and early May had lifted the spirits of the Somerset folk who, like the rest of Britain, were still in post war depression and had just experienced one of the hardest winters on record.

People are basically the same everywhere, and their main concerns are having a job and a roof over their heads. Being on the winning side of the longest and most cruel World War ever, could make those who survived it feel that they somehow deserved more from life, and when many men came back from the battlefields to find that their everyday lives were even poorer and harder than before, then petty grievances could often grow into more serious grudges, and these grudges could boil over into violence, especially when fuelled by alcohol. Everyone has heard of Cheddar Cheese, but a stranger should be wary of Somerset cider, especially the sort that most pubs sold until it was deemed too potent. Brewed in many isolated farmhouses, this was not the sweet, bottled drink that was so refreshing on a hot day, but a rough tackle that was yellow in colour, and almost green.

The three youths who tumbled out of the public bar of The Post had learned to drink during the war years, and although they were too young to have been called up for hostilities, they knew that they would soon have to present themselves for peacetime conscription. Two of the lads were apprentice miners, and lived as neighbours in the back-to-back cottages in Hollow Down. The third boy George was not from Somerset at all; he hailed from London and had been evacuated to Somerset during the war. George Millard was an orphan, and the only relative that he knew of was a much older brother who was a soldier, and had been killed "somewhere in Southern Europe".

The three youngsters had been drinking steadily, but they could still recite the boring age-old local refrain:

"Beer on cider makes a good rider".

"Cider on beer makes you feel queer".

As they turned right to walk up to Hollow Down, they hadn't quite got to the state of feeling queer, but as they bawled out the two lines of the rhyme, they felt like Jack the Lads who could please any local girl. However there were no girls about on this dark night as they stumbled home, but then Alan, the youngest boy, squinted his eyes and said, "What the bloody hell is that?"

Then, seeing a figure of a man approaching, he shouted, "Bugger me, who's this?"

As he got closer, the tall swarthy looking man attempted to cross over to the other side of the lane, but Alan called out "Where bist goin' Mister? We bain't gonna bite thee!"

Alan and his workmate Derek looked at each other puzzled, but the more aggressive George caught the stranger by the shoulder as he put his head down and tried to walk away. "What's wrong?" he said, swaying drunkenly, "we not good enough for thee?"

The man turned around to face the three and said in a foreign accent, "Please, I have hurry, let me alone".

"He's a bloody foreigner!" shouted George in his Cockney/Somerset accent, "What you doin' around here mate?"

George still had his hand on the stranger's shoulder and tried to turn him around to face him, but as he did so the man swung his right arm in a low arc and slashed a knife towards the youth's stomach. George gasped, then groaned, before vomiting on the road and sinking to his knees. He soon realized that he wasn't badly hurt, but looked a fool in front of his friends who seemed unable to take in what had happened, stuck on the spot. The stranger started to run in the direction he had come from, and George, recovering, shouted, "Get the bastard, don't let him get away".

"He's got a knife," said Alan.

"Not now he hasn't, he's thrown the bloody thing away, look." Derek had seen the knife blade flash, even in the poor light, and heard it fall.

The man got to the Hollow Down crossroads and took the right turn in the direction of Midsomer Hollow, running as fast as he could. He could hear the two youngsters gaining on him, so when he got to the entrance of Hollow Hall Cottages he ran up the track a short way before hiding behind a tree. George had almost caught up with the two drunken labourers, and called for them to wait. He was lucky that the point of the knife had only scratched him and ripped his jacket.

"I reckon that bastard is a wop, them eyeties killed me brother".

The night was quiet and dark, but the three fanned out and they knew that the foreigner didn't have many places to hide. George reckoned himself to be tough, but if he hadn't been drunk he might have swallowed his pride and stepped wide of this fit, older man. As it was his blood was up, and it was his idea to search the track.

The man heard them coming, and made the mistake of leaving his hiding place behind the dark tree. He ran up the track towards the cottages, but the three soon caught up to him and George jumped on his back, bringing him down. Shouting drunken obscenities, they cowardly kicked the supposed Italian who tried to protect his head with his hands.

"You picked on the wrong one, Wop," sneered the ignorant farm labourer, and stood back to get a full swing of his boot into the man's head. Hopelessly outnumbered, the foreigner suffered several more vicious kicks from the youth, one of them breaking his bloodied fingers that were covering his face. The stranger gave a low moan, and seemed to sink further into the ground. The youths stood back looking, and Alan stuttered, "He's bloody unconscious, better leave him."

"Serves the bastard right," replied George, "But bollocks to leaving him, he might report us."

"He's not moving," said Derek timidly, "Have you killed him George?"

"Me, you little shit, me? You mean *we* don't you? We all pitched in. Here, feel his pulse. See if it's going." They didn't really know where a pulse was, and certainly none of the three had seen a dead person in their lives, but they were frightened now.

After a few minutes the man still hadn't stirred and Derek started to snivel: "He's dead, what we gonna do? I didn't mean to kill 'im George, but you kept on kicking."

George was frightened too, but he wasn't going to show it to these yokels, "Alright we've killed the bugger, but we can't leave him here, we'll have to put him somewhere." Just then they heard a train whistle, and the killers remembered how close they were to the railway.

"Let's carry him across the grounds and throw him on the lines, they'll think it was an accident or summit."

This was Alan who had found his voice, and was just as shaken as Derek. In their panic, the youths just wanted to get rid of the body and go home.

"Good idea Al," said George, "And it were your idea, don't forget. We be all in this together, right? I said right, Derek?"

Derek nodded crazily and said, "Yes, yes, let's get rid of him."

A couple of fields behind Hollow Hall Cottages was the deep cutting of the Somerset and Dorset Railway, just before it enters the Eastcompton Tunnel. Two of the youths carried the dead man by his arms, while the third supported his legs. After a while their burden became too heavy for them in their half-drunken state, so they dragged the body the rest of the way until they came to the top of the steep bank. The Pines Express had passed by a couple of hours earlier, so there probably wouldn't be any more trains that night as they heaved the body down the embankment. They saw it roll over the primroses that looked so colourful and peaceful in the daytime, and come to a stop, with part of it lying on the rails. They then ran for their lives for home, not giving a thought to alibis, left evidence, or remorse for what they had done.

While the three frightened young men passed by the darkened Hollow Hall Cottages again, the drug-induced Ken Dimmock pulled himself up from his bed to look out of the dirt-grimed window...

CHAPTER 2

The body was seen by the next early morning train driver, but not quick enough for him to avoid hitting the dead man a glancing blow.

Jack Snow was driving the up express and had just swooped through the tunnel on his way to Midsomer Hollow South Station, and eventually on to Bath. It took Jack a long way to pull up the powerful Standard 9F, and a runner was sent back to Eastcompton signal box to report the incident.

Jack and his fireman were joined by the train's guard, and between them they managed to extract the mangled body from under the carriage wheels and pull it to the side of the track where they covered it with a blanket. In the cool early morning air the dormant locomotive stood there with steam escaping and metallic noises coming from its cooling parts. Like a huge panting beast, the steep sides of the cutting reverberated with the engine's exhaust note.

It was a good half an hour before the train was given permission to proceed to Midsomer Hollow, but the guard and one other man were to stay with the dead man until the police arrived, bringing the driver and fireman back with them.

Jack and his young fireman Billy Hughes arrived back at the scene in company with a constable and a police doctor. Dr Buell was not strictly a police doctor as such, as he had his own practice in Midsomer Hollow, but he was called out occasionally by the local police in emergencies such as this. After looking at the body Dr Buell asked the driver where exactly it had been lying, but Snow was beginning to feel the effects of his traumatic experience, and looked ill. Billy however was young and eager, and was hoping for promotion one day to driver when he was old enough and had enough experience. "He was lying on 'is right side Sir", he volunteered to the doctor.

"And the train hit him…?"

"Well Sir, it was 'is 'ead and right shoulder which was lying on the rails like, and we hit 'un on the left side," replied Billy a little more uncertainly.

"Quite," muttered the doctor.

"Look here Doctor," Constable Scott suddenly shouted, "There's blood here on the bank."

A few people had gathered at the top of the embankment looking down, no doubt farm workers who had heard the noises. "All down here Doctor, looks like he rolled down the hill. Even the primroses have blood on them."

"Hmm," replied the doctor looking up, "Or *was* rolled down the hill. You had better call for reinforcements constable, and stop those people from getting too close."

Doctor Buell looked in the man's now tattered jacket for some identification. He could see that the dead man had been well dressed before his untimely end. "Well," he exclaimed, "This man is Italian constable, here is his passport."

The passport photo showed a good-looking, swarthy man of Mediterranean appearance, with very dark hair plastered down and with a military style small black moustache. Looking again at the mangled face, the doctor was experienced enough to see that the photo was probably his.

"Well, this is out of our hands now I would say, constable. We have an alien person here, and possibly foul play."

"Of course Doctor," replied Scott, "I'll go along to Eastcompton Box and get them to call out the Bath Police."

While they were waiting for help to arrive, the dead body was lifted on to the small shunter engine that had brought the men back from Midsomer Hollow Station.

"Where do 'ee think the Italian came from Sir?" Billy asked the constable. He had a habit of calling anyone in authority Sir.

"That's what we'll have to find out," replied the constable dryly.

"'Ee be probably from the school up in Stanten." This was from driver Snow who was recovering a bit from his shock.

"The school?" asked Doctor Buell, in his own public school accent.

"Aye, they have some of them foreigners working there for the monks as far as I bin told." Constable Scott nodded and put it: "Ah, he means up Downbury School, Doctor. But what would this man be doing around these parts?"

Downbury was a Benedictine Abbey and Private Boarding School, the second largest Catholic one in Europe. Most of the teachers there were monks, and the Abbey was also home to the priests who presided over the several rural parishes in the area. Although Downbury employed a lot of local people from the village of Stanten-on-the-Fosse where it was situated, they also had some foreign workers, mostly Irish and Italian, who worked as waiters or kitchen staff as a rule.

Constable Scott had set off to send his call which found the Eastcompton staff and station in a state of high excitement. Word was already getting round the local villages about the gruesome discovery on their railway, and everyone was hungry for news. Scott had taken the dead man's passport with him and relayed its details to Bath Police, who told him to wait for a reply and that assistance was on the way. Provisional enquiries were made to the Italian Consulate.

"The call came back from Bath, and Scott was handed the phone. "Is that PC Scott?" an official voice asked.

"Yes sir, Scott here."

"Then listen Scott, I'm Inspector Markham. Did you say you think there is foul play here?"

"I do Sir. You will no doubt be coming out yourself?"

"No Constable, some of our men should be with you soon, and when they arrive I want you to assist them in roping off the entire area. I understand there is a track leading to some cottages nearby? Well, the track is to be sealed off until the people from London arrive."

Scott was surprised. "London Sir, is it that serious?"

"Could be constable. Keep this to yourself, but our enquiries have turned up that this man's passport is forged, and that he may not even be an Italian!"

CHAPTER 3

Coming away from the site of the railway cutting and across a couple of fields are Hollow Hall Cottages, a small terrace of stone-built dwellings owned by the local landowner Guy Beechcroft. A track leads down to Hollow Lane, and if you turn left the road will take you straight on to Midsomer Hollow, and as you start to descend the hill at Silver Street the railway station is just on the left. Turning right from the track leads to the precarious Hollow Down Crossroads, where drivers would often take their lives in their hands by going right for Eastcompton, straight ahead for Stanten, or left for Hollow Down and the main Fosseway. Before coming to the crossroads there is also a slip road off to the left that comes out just before Hollow Down Chapel over on the other side of the road. All these roads and lanes are lined by tall, thick horse chestnut and beech trees, giving the area a kind of secluded and sinister feel.

By midday the immediate area was sealed off, including access to the track. By mid-afternoon two MI5 agents arrived to take control of the investigation. The reason why Scotland Yard had passed this crime on to MI5 was that it involved the possible murder of a subject from a foreign country, and that a man had been found dead with a fake passport in his possession. Feelings were still running high in those early post-war years, and security had been upped due to the London Conference that had started in February of 1948. London was full of spies, even within the Foreign Office, so the Somerset affair had a mild importance at that moment. For this reason the two agents sent weren't particularly senior, but Detective Harris and Jr Detective Cartwright were pleased to get the assignment and to be able to leave the capital for a while.

Bill Harris was very tall and slim, and had a prominent, military style moustache that gave him a serious look. Tim Cartwright on the other hand had fair, wavy hair and a handsome, young-looking face.

While Harris went to inspect the body at the mortuary, Cartwright was given the job of interviewing the occupants of Hollow Hall Cottages, and finding out if anyone else had seen or heard anything the night before.

Ken Dimmock was brought back to the UK late in 1945, a man broken in health and mind. Detached to the 1st Battalion of the Somerset Light Infantry, Ken had been taken prisoner in Burma, and had suffered unspeakable torment as a POW of the Japanese. Skeleton-thin and racked with malaria, Ken was too ill to be repatriated straight away after the Japanese surrender, and spent several months recuperating in an Australian hospital. His doctor knew he couldn't live much longer, and the patient received regular shots of morphine to ease his pain and to help him sleep. Ken's house was at the end of a terrace near to the track, and his bed had been pulled close to the window so that he could look out on to it.

Tim Cartwright was told all this by Ken's wife Alice, and Tim promised not to tire her husband out, but just wanted to ask him a few questions. Climbing the narrow and curving staircase, Tim had a morbid thought in wondering how they would manage to carry a coffin up and down here.

"Perhaps they will carry him down and put him in the box downstairs," he thought to himself, then quickly turned his mind from it.

"Hello Ken, my name is Cartwright and I am down here from London investigating a missing person, a foreigner. I know that you haven't been feeling well lately, but wondered if you had heard or seen anything strange lately. Especially last night?"

"Only the chariot son, always the chariot," replied Ken in a surprisingly clear voice.

"The chariot?" asked the young detective. "I don't understand Ken."

Dimmock could only be around thirty-five, but looked twenty years older. Tim tried another tack, "I hear you were in Burma Ken, in The Somersets?"

Ken's face was wet with perspiration, even though the day was quite cool. "You don't believe me, do you?" he responded, "No-one believes me, but I see it nearly every night."

"You see a chariot Ken, what sort of chariot?" Ken's face had gone even whiter, and he held on to Tim's shoulder, squeezing it.

"A Roman chariot, man... it's all white and shining and there is a soldier riding it. It goes all round Hollow Down and then it comes..."

"Comes where Ken?" asked Tim.

"It comes up the track. I think it's looking for me."

Tim was convinced the man was near crazy, or perhaps just under the influence of the morphine. He loosened the man's hold on his shoulder and made to leave, but as he turned away Ken's voice called him back.

"I'm not mad son, if that's what you think, but I do see these things and they frighten me."

"Of course Ken," said Cartwright, "I have had hallucinations myself when I have had a temperature, everyone does."

"I did see something last night," he suddenly blurted out. It was as if he had got over his spell of madness and was now lucid.

"What was it?" asked the MI5 agent.

"I heard noises like people was fighting outside on the track, so I got up and looked out the window."

"And?" prompted Cartwright.

"I thought it was the chariot again so I hid my face, but I saw some men carrying something. It was dark and I couldn't see much."

"Did you know any of the men?" asked Tim.

"Aye, I think one of them was that youngster who works on the farm. He's not from around here..."

Ken's hands were shaking. "Sit down son, give me one of them fags," he said pointing to his woodbines on the table.

"Do you think you should?" replied the agent.

"Damn, I haven't got much else to look forward to, have one yourself."

Tim lit both their smokes and waited for Ken to speak.

"Is it serious, what you are investigating?" he asked.

Cartwright thought before answering. "Well yes, a man has been found dead, down on the railway. We think he may have been killed first and then taken there. Why Ken? Do you know the other men you saw?"

Ken took a deep drag on his cigarette and coughed, bringing tears to his eyes.

"Aye, I did, I saw Derek Bull my younger cousin, but he's no killer Mister, he's a nice lad."

Mrs Dimmock was waiting at the bottom of the stairs when the detective came down. She was a pretty looking woman in her early thirties, rather plump, and with her wavy hair worn shoulder length.

Tim said to her, "What is all this about the Roman chariot, Mrs Dimmock?"

"Oh, he's been saying he's seen it for months now, but I reckon it's them drugs be making him see things. He baint a liar though, not Ken Sir."

"Does anyone else come to see him," he asked, "Except the doctor?"

"Well the minister from the chapel do come up to sit with him twice a week," Ken's wife replied.

"I noticed a chapel down by the crossroads. Is Ken a Methodist?"

"Well," replied Mrs Dimmock, "He were christened C of E, but you understand round here where it be a bit isolated like, you go to wherever is nearest. Except if it be Catholic of course. Not that they would want to come to our chapel neither." She laughed good-humouredly.

"Would the minister be in the chapel now?" asked Tim. Mrs Dimmock looked at the large clock on her mantlepiece and replied that probably at this time of day, yes.

Tim walked down to the chapel that was situated just off the Post crossroads, and entered the open door. He saw a woman with a yellow duster in her hand, who was arranging some flowers in a bowl.

"Excuse me," said the agent. "Could you tell me if the minister is here?"

"I can, and I am she," replied the young woman.

Cartwright's mouth fell open, and he just stared.

"You obviously haven't read Adam Bede," she teased. "You know, a female preacher!"

"Yes, yes sorry," said the MI5 man. "I was just surprised to find that the minister is a woman."

"Pleasantly surprised," he added with a smile.

"Thank you, my name is Marjorie, Marjorie Knight. And you are?"

"I am Tim Cartwright, and I'm a sort of policeman," he answered.

Marjorie was a very attractive woman in her mid-thirties, and had been minister there for nearly two years. "Sort of?" she asked.

"Well," said Cartwright, "I am in the security services and am investigating a suspicious person who isn't from these shores"

"Ah," smiled Marjorie, "you are after a spy! How exciting!"

Tim smiled too and asked her, "I understand you know Ken Dimmock Miss Knight, and you visit him?"

"Please call me Marjorie," she replied. "Everyone else does. Yes, Ken is a lovely man, and has suffered so much, like many other people. Why do you ask?"

"He confided some information to me, and also mentioned a cousin of his, Derek. Would you know him too?"

"Oh yes, he's not in any trouble I hope. They are a nice family," she explained.

"I'm afraid he could be. These, these hallucinations that Ken has... does he tell you about them?"

"About the Roman chariot that drives all around The Post and Hollow Down at night and ends up coming up the drive to his house? Yes, but Mr Cartwright, when he is lucid, Ken is a very intelligent man."

"Return me the compliment please and call me Tim," he laughed. "Yes, I thought so. Well, I must be carrying on now, it's been more than a pleasure meeting you Marjorie."

He gave her his hand.

"For me too Tim. Tell me, you are Welsh aren't you? Are you of the faith?"

Tim put on an exaggerated Welsh accent and replied that he was indeed, and that all his family were chapel folk.

"Splendid," replied Miss Knight, "Perhaps you can attend a service here some time?"

"I will certainly try," he said, waving his goodbye.

"Oh, by the way," he said turning back. "A bit melancholy this, but I notice there is no cemetery here."

"No," replied Marjorie. "Interment would normally be in Stanten, in their C of E Church."

"Tim," she said again pondering, "I read somewhere once that when people are taking strong drugs or painkillers or are... well, near death... they sometimes have the ability to see things that could turn out to be... I don't know, prophecies or omens maybe."

"And you think that the visions Ken has could be a sort of warning of forthcoming doom?" asked the Junior Detective. Then, before she could answer he followed up with: "Perhaps we can discuss this further over lunch one day... or dinner?"

"That would be nice," replied Marjorie, and Tim went off with a spring in his step, promising to be in touch.

A constable reported later on that a knife had been found at the side of Hollow Lane, and this was taken to Bath for fingerprinting. Furthermore, blood had been found on the track where the violent attack had taken place, and there were clear signs that something heavy had been dragged across the fields. The investigation seemed to be going well, and by the evening the three youths had been interrogated, arrested, and taken to Bath police station.

Detective Bill Harris had also had a busy and fruitful day. The fingerprints on the knife, and the blood found both matched that of the dead man. Harris was an experienced investigator, and went through all the man's belongings thoroughly. He relayed this to Cartwright when his assistant arrived in Bath.

"And Tim," he said, "There is more. I found this stitched into the hem of the man's jacket."

"What is it Sir?"

Harris handed him a grubby folded card, something that looked official or military.

"This is the guy's *real* identity card. He looks to me to be either an army officer or a diplomat. Tim, this man isn't Italian at all, he is Spanish!"

CHAPTER 4

"I think it's high time we had a word with Downbury," said Harris. They were in Bath police station, and he asked the operator there to put him through to the school.

The Bursar answered, and Bill said, "Good morning, my name is Harris and I am calling from Bath Police. Can you tell me please if you have had a Spanish gentleman staying at the school recently?"

"Do you mean working here? Umm sergeant Harris is it?" asked the Bursar.

"Just Detective Harris. Well working, or just staying there?"

The Bursar said he would check up and call back, which he did 10 minutes later. "Yes sir, a gentleman came about a week ago, but he went off to London as far as I know. His room was still being kept for him".

"Was?"

"Yes Sir", replied the Bursar cautiously.

"Do you know what his business was in your school?", pried Harris.

"Well I am not sure Sir, but he seemed to be a personal friend of one of our priests here. Why, is there a problem? I am sure he must have had his travel visa in order".

"Do you know which priest he was friendly with?" asked the agent, ignoring the question.

"Well yes Sir, it seemed he knew the Abbot", replied the Bursar, not knowing if he should have said that or not.

"Really?, said Harris, "well can you please tell the Abbot that this Spanish gentleman has been found dead, and that my partner and I would like to visit him this afternoon".

The Bursar answered that he thought that would be difficult, but added "Would you like to speak to him now Sir? I can put you through to his office".

"Yes, Mr Harris this man indeed came to Downbury", said the church leader, taking the call.

"As your guest Sir?", asked Agent Harris.

"Yes, he requested to stay for a while as he needed a base".

"How did he die?", asked the Abbot.

"We think he died as the result of a brawl. Tell me Abbot, did you know that this gentleman was carrying a false Italian passport? Did you know him from before?"

"No Mr Harris, I had never met him before", replied the Abbot, rather cautiously thought Harris.

"And you thought he was an Italian?"

"No, said the priest after a pause, "his real name, as you probably know is Juan Galvez Moreno, and he is Spanish, a retired Spanish general in fact".

"I see, said Harris, looking at his partner Cartwright, "and may I ask what his business was with you Sir?"

"That was private Mr Harris, I don't think I can....."

"My companion and I are from MI5 Sir, cut in Harris, "and we have been sent down from London to investigate this death. Anything you tell us will be in confidence of course, but we must ask you to tell us everything you know. Spain is not one of this country's allies at the moment as you know. Now, one of their military personnel has been found dead here carrying a false passport, and apparently he was an aquaintance of yours?"

"Yes, Mr Harris of course. I am only thinking of the reputation of Downbury...."

"Is there something you know that could damage that reputation?, asked the detective. "Apart from people finding out that this person wasn't who he was pretending to be?", he added.

The Abbot replied in a firm voice, "General Galvez told me he was an envoy from the Caudillo".

"General Franco?", asked Harris surprised,

"Indeed, replied the churchman, "he confided in me that the Generalissimo has plans for the future to bring back the monarchy in Spain, and that he is grooming someone for the role of King. This person is still young, and Franco is tentatively interested in him spending part of his education here. You know, learning English. Sr Galvez thinks it a good idea. We have a long tradition of young Catholic Royals studying here from all over the world you know Mr Harris. Galvez told me he had other important business in London. I assure you I knew nothing of any subterfuge".

"You are not above the law though Father, and you may have technically broken it. Are you sure you don't know anything else about this man's business? It seems a pretty flimsy excuse to put himself and you in danger for. Do you have some connection with Spain perhaps?".

A longer pause, and then the Abbot replied, "I think perhaps we should meet Mr Harris. As I said before, my prime concern is for the discretion of Downbury. Would you please phone me to let me know when you will come?"

Harris answered in the affirmative, but he advised that part of his team would be visiting the school beforehand, and requested that they be given free rein to inspect the deceased's room.

Harris had just put the phone down when he was told of a call for him on another line, from a member of the Forensics team at Hollow Down.

"Sir, we have firm footprints of the deceased on the damp parts of the track, after the area where we think he was attacked".

"Must have been from when they stood him up perhaps?"

"No Sir, said the specialist, "there are samples of his footprints all the way to the embankment of the railway. He had very large feet, I would say a continental size 46".

"I will be right over, looks like he had been up that track before then?", said Harris.

"And back again of course, there are prints facing in both directions".

Before leaving, Detective Harris instructed Junior Detective Cartwright and a CID officer from Bath to start interrogating the three youths seperately.

Weighed down by the importance of what they had done, Derek and Alan soon talked. Derek broke down and sobbed "We were pissed Sir, and when he knifed George we ran after him and found him up the track, but we didn't mean to kill him".
Although not trying to save their own skins, under interrogation they both admitted that Millard was a violent type, and that they tended to go along with him.

"What will happen to us Sir, will they hang us?, asked a terrified Alan.

Cartwright shook his head and said, "I don't think so son, but that may depend on how well you can keep your mouths shut".

Harris drove back to Hollow Down in a radio car, and a call was put through to him from one of the local officers at Downbury.

"Sergeant Biggs here Sir. We've checked the man's room thoroughly, and have found the usual suitcase and clothes, and under his mattress there was quite a lot of notes hidden, about 1000 pounds worth we think, and together with the money were 2 single flight tickets for Buenos Aries. One way tickets".

"Interesting Sergeant, very interesting. said Harris, "What date is the flight?".

"Well it seems to be for tomorrow".

"You have done very well Sergeant, thank you", said the MI5 man.

"That's not all though Sir, we showed the Abbot a photo taken of the dead man, and he swears it isn`t the same person who came to see him", replied Sgt. Biggs.

"And he doesn't know who that person is?", said Harris surprised.

"No he doesn't, but the Bursar may. Apparently this Galvez was held up in London at a conference, and asked a friend of his with whom he was travelling back to Spain to collect the few clothes for him that he had left in his room in Downbury. The Bursar took the phone call from the man, and he asked if he could stay in the room himself for two nights, before going back up to London to catch a flight to Madrid with Sr Galvez".

"And because he was a friend of the friend of the Abbot, he agreed I suppose?", asked Harris, a little pointedly.

"He did, and there were no questions asked. The Bursar can`t even remember if he asked the Spaniard his name", said Biggs.

"So what were the man's movements? Did he say?".

"Yes Sir, replied the Bath Sergeant, "the Bursar said he arrived mid morning with a small holdall and briefcase of his own, was shown to his room, and then went out somewhere later on".

"And did he sleep in his room that night?", asked Harris.

"No Sir he didn't, but then he wouldn't have seeing as he was killed. The dates coincide".

"Hmmmm", muttered Harris pensively, "Well thanks again Sergeant, I hope to see you soon".

Bill Harris lit up one of his Players, and asked his driver to put him through to Tim Cartwright in Bath. Briefly bringing his assistant up to date, he asked Cartwright to call MI5 headquarters in London to advise them of their Somerset investigations, and to see what links they may have from other areas, if any.

"I'm coming back to Bath now Tim, tell London I want any news they have in about half an hour".

There was no call from London when Harris returned to Bath Police Station, so he and Harris went to a cafe round the corner for a spot of lunch.'
Bath was a busy city, as well as being a beautiful one, and the noise of the shoppers and commuters mingled with that of the steam trains serving its two railway stations.

"So what do you think Sir?", asked Cartwright.

"Well this Somerset air gives me an appetite, smiled Harris, cutting into his meat pie, "let's eat first before that call comes through".

Harris offered Tim one of his cigarettes and lit them both. Stirring his tea, he was deep in thought so Cartwright waited for him to speak.

"What we have Tim is a Spaniard who has been killed and was travelling as someone else, who probably pretended that he was a friend of General Galvez, who somehow found out that Galvez had friends in Downbury, and undoubtedly used that for his advantage. He had air tickets for Argentina hidden in Galvez's room in Downbury, and a stash of cash. Now where did he get that cash from? Why was he presumably making a bunk, and, if he only wanted the room for a couple of nights to hide out in, why did he go out at all to put himself at risk? And what was he doing up a dark track in Hollow Down at that time of night?".

"A lot of questions, replied Cartwright, tapping his ash into the tray, "and here's another one Sir. What would have happened if this man hadn't been killed by those kids. I mean, if a crime has been committed somewhere, then surely we should hear about it soon?"

"Obviously that's the reason why our man was about to fly. Apparently the air tickets were reservations for a flight to Buenos Aries, but not actual tickets, so we don't know the name of the person travelling with him. I think the answers to most of our questions will come from London Tim. Let's go back to the station".

CHAPTER 5

The Duke of Avila was spending his second term of office as Spain's representative to the UK. While not exactly Spain's Ambassador, he was extended almost the same level of position, and his office and lifestyle in London was one that a man of his stature and personal wealth appreciated and expected. Avila was an Anglophile, and as such was replaced in London by General Franco in the early years of World War 11 for someone who was more sympathetic to Nazi Germany and the Axis powers. As the tide of the war turned in the Allies favour however, the wily General brought back the handsome, dashing Duke to his former role. Indeed, in the immediate post war years Franco found his regime increasingly isolated in the world. Russia wanted the USA and Britain to invade Spain in 1945 to end what Stalin thought was the last bastion of Fascism. After the death of Roosevelt, the new President Harry Truman wasn't as kindly toward Franco as his predecessor had been, and even Winston Churchill had been ousted as Britain voted in a Socialist Prime Minister. The Labour Party's Clement Atlee had become Britain's first ever Deputy Prime Minister in the wartime coalition government, and was nobody's fool. Like Churchill, Truman and most of their Allies, he knew that the real danger now came not from Fascism, but from the Soviets and the spread of Communism. General Franco was ruling his country with an iron fist, but he would fight Communism with every last breath in his body.

Up until 1946 the defeated Spanish Republic had moved it's government to Mexico where Diego Martinez Barrio became it's President, but now they were based in Paris, and Alvaro de Albornoz y Liminia had become their Prime Minister.

At the end of the Spanish Civil War in 1939 Neville Chamberlain, the British PM, had almost no option but to accept General Franco's regime as the official government of Spain. From then on the Republic's influence grew less and less, although they still possessed a very good intelligence system, and would do all in their power to damage Franco and his relationship with the rest of the world.

The London Conference of April 1948 was a post war meeting of the victorious allies, and their main agenda was to finalise plans for Germany, and for Berlin. Joseph Stalin of course, would be taking his usual tough stance on behalf of Soviet Russia, and his recent annexation of Czechoslovakia was a warning to the West, and a worry to General Franco.

The Caudillo was sending an envoy to London to speak to the Duke of Avila - Juan Galvez Moreno, who was a General, and who had been one of Franco's most trusted military advisors during the Civil War. Galvez Moreno's task now was to prime up Avila for his participation in the London Conference, should he be invited, and to put forward Spain's arguments in asking for US/UK financial aid, and for help in the defence of their borders should it be necessary.

Although General Franco wasn't about to plead for Spain's entry into the UN or any other organisation, he was confident that he could obtain the concessions that he needed. Juan Galvez Moreno was also a messenger, and what he was carrying with him assured Spain's wish to be heard.

The Duke of Avila was an amateur at politics, he left difficult decisions to others, and enjoyed his life in London as a fairly rich and privileged representative. Post war Britain was still gloomy and rationing was widespread, but Spain was in a much worse condition. The Duke's wife and family were able to come over to see him every few months or so, and he had a good social life where he often wined and dined with friends. There were other Spanish people living in London of course, and the beautiful Arancha was one of them.

Arancha's apartment in Chelsea wasn't directly paid for by the Duke, or by any other politician or client for that matter, but her rent certainly came from their pockets.

Soberly dressed in a white blouse and black skirt, Arancha had her thick, black hair tied back, but this didn't make her look much older than her thirty years.

She opened the door to the bashful looking Duke, and, pointing to her bedroom, simply said, "In there".

Telling the older man to stand at the foot of her bed, Arancha sat on a chair and crossed her legs, giving him a view of her lovely, shapely thighs.

"And what have you been up to *Carlito*?, she purred, "I heard that you haven't been behaving yourself lately"

"No Mistress", he replied lamely.

"Then you will have to be punished, won't you Carlos?"

The Duke felt himself stiffening even more, and Arancha stood up, bending forward so that he could see down her cleavage. The top buttons of her blouse were open, and he could see her firm breasts nestling in the white, lacy bra.

"Over the bed", she ordered, and went to open her wardrobe.

When Arancha turned around, she had a wicked looking rattan school cane which she bent in her hands to show how supple it was. She swished it through the air and said, "Five I think will do it".

Although Anglophiles, Mistress and Sub probably thought metric, so the usual British *six of the best* would seem excessive!

Arancha swished the cane down across the Duke's backside five times, then laughed and threw the cane on the bed.

The Duke thought she was a good sport, and when he felt in a less submissive mood had more than once taken her over his knee, pulled her knickers down and given her a good spanking himself!

She lay back on the bed and beckoned him to her with her finger. "What would your wife say if she knew?", she asked, but was really saying to herself "*Madre mia, todo por dinero*".

The Duke lay down next to her, her perfume filling his nostrils.

"Well, I will tell you when I see her", he laughed, and started to undress her.

CHAPTER 6

Juan Pardo left Paris for London on 14th April, travelling on a 14 day visa and passport in his own name, but with the forged Italian one in Bruno Calvetti's name.

Pardo's colleagues and employers had made a good job of his forged papers, but when they rubber stamped his mission to London, little did they know to what extremes he would be prepared to go. He would be well paid though, and the job should give him personal satisfaction. Pardo knew what day Franco's envoy Galvez Moreno was arriving in England. He knew that he would be going from London Airport to Paddington Station, and then catching a train down to Bath. From here he would presumably be catching a local train, or taxi to the small Somerset village where he would be staying temporarly, before travelling back to London to speak to his government's representative there. Juan Pardo was well informed, and best of all, he knew what Galvez Moreno would be carrying in his briefcase.

"Very well, he had said to himself when planning his movements, "we will see El General "en Londres".

Galvez Moreno was received at Downbury with great courtesy, where he stayed for one night, and then in the morning the school's chauffeur drove him to Bath Railway Station. The Spanish general left a few of his belongings in his room, and intended calling back to stay in the peaceful Somerset countryside for a few more days, once his business in London was terminated.

The 18th April was the day that the Spanish Representative in London was due to meet the Caudillo's envoy. The Duke of Avila didn't have official Embassy status, so he received General Galvez Moreno in his private office. The two had not met before officially, but had seen photos of each other.

The Duke greeted the general warmly, shaking his hand with an informal *"Hola Juan, como estas?"*

"I am well Duke, thank you", replied the other.

"Sit down please, would you like a coffee perhaps?".

The Duke's visitor sat down, but declined the offer of coffee.

Keen to start their business, the Duke asked if the general had the document.

"I have this one Sir, shall I read it to you", the general asked rather strangely.

"Well yes of course, but the text shouldn't have changed", replied Avila surprised.

His guest said nothing, then started to read the official looking document he had extracted from his briefcase.

"We the undersigned, being representatives of the Spanish Republican Government in Exile, wish to draw your attention to the information and facts that are outlined in this document, and desire that you will take into consideration these matters when discussing the future of the Rebel Fascist Government of General Franco.

We have irrefutable proof of the location of several mass graves in Extremadura that hold the bodies of several thousand soldiers executed by the Nationalist forces between the years 1936-1939, and that at least one thousand of these souls are of those that fought for The International Brigade, including British and Irish subjects.

Furthermore, we have in our possession two signed statements from women who were passengers on a British steamship that was attacked from the air off Barcelona in 1939. This was a wholly unprovoked and vicious attack by the Nationalist forces, and only the bravery of the ship's crew prevented the ship from being sunk or captured".

The Duke listened unbelievingly, and said sharply, "But was is this Galvez? This is preposterous, and rubbish. Where did you get this from, have you intercepted it?"

"No Sir, replied the Spaniard, "I haven't intercepted it, I have brought it with me, from Paris, from our Government!".

"Your government Galvez? Good God, who are you? Where is the document you were instructed to bring me?"

"You had better sit down Señor, sneered the other, "or does your *culo* hurt too much?"

"What damned insolence, stormed the Duke, "I'm going to call the police".

"I wouldn't do that Duke if I were you, said the visitor, "not if you want to see Arancha alive again. Oh yes, she is being taken care of, but she has been very *useful* to us".

"You aren't Galvez Moreno, who the hell are you?", said Avila exasperated.

"Oh but I am Don Carlos, sneered the supposed envoy, "here is my passport. See, a very good likeness I think you will agree?"

"I don't understand any of this, what do you want from me?", bellowed the Spanish nobleman.

"We are getting to that Duke. For the moment, all you need to know that is if you don't follow my instructions the body of a member of the Spanish Republic will soon be found, a man whose signature was one of those on that document I have just shown you. Copies of that document have been sent to members of the Russian Delegation here for the London Conference, and also to certain *sympathetic* Labour Party members".

"But you are crazy, do you really think that these, these fabrications, will turn people against Franco? Now, more than ever the Western Powers need allies against the spread of communism. Russia have already annexed Czechoslovakia. If the Republic have sent you here on this errand, then they are wasting their time", replied the Duke smiling thinly.

"You miss the point my dear Sir, smirked the stranger, "when this man's body is found and identified as one of the signaturees, who do you think the police will suspect of being responsible for his elimination? Are not your fingerprints in Arancha's room, on the glass you drank from for example? Oh yes, my colleague and I know all about your last visit to Arancha. Your wife would be interested to know about your *kinks*, let alone El Caudillo. What would he think of his representative visiting whores and leaving himself open to threats?"

"Hijo de puta", stormed the Duke, "so that's it, blackmail. So what do you scum want me to do, act treasonably towards my government? Resign from my position maybe? How do I know you are telling me the truth anyway?.

"Oh it is the truth Don Carlos, smiled the other, and took a wicked looking knife from the inside pocket of his coat. "Juan Galvez Moreno's body is in Arancha's apartment right now, and she is being held until my business with you is complete".

The Duke made a move to stand up, but the other was quicker.

"I wouldn't do anything silly Duke, he sneered, "I am a trained assassin and could kill you before you get halfway across this room".

"Damn you, replied the Duke, "I don't care one bit about this rubbish you have sent from these so called sympathisers of yours, and Arancha is just a whore. If you have frightened her into implicating me in your filthy murder, then I tell you that the British police aren't stupid".

"No they aren't Duke, and neither are the British Government. Don't forget that Galvez Moreno's main errand here was to bring back the 1940 Agreement".

The Duke of Avila's face fell. He went pale and said with an effort, "So you and your henchman have killed Galvez Moreno, you have changed identities with him.....”

“You must agree that we are very alike”, cut in the imposter.

The Duke continued, “And now you have the Agreement in your dirty hands. You won’t get away with this, I tell you, your Spanish Republic is dead and buried”.

“Perhaps you are right my Duke, replied the other suspiciously, “it could be time to make the best of a bad job. Here is our proposal, or if you like, our ultimatum”.

The Duke was trying to get all these details and threats in some kind of order in is head. He was in trouble, that was clear, and it looked for the moment as if he was trapped into listening to this despicable man. He waited for the other to start.

“I know the following text of the Agreement of 1940 off by heart my Duke”, and he related:

”His Majesty’s Government hereby give notice that they formally recognise the Nationialist Government of Spain, and that they accept General Francisco Franco Bahamonde as it’s leader.

Furthermore, his Majesty’s Government would like to stress that they implicitly kept a neutral stance during Spain’s recent three years of civil war.

Now, the roles are reversed as Britain finds itself in a state of war against Nazi Germany and her Axis partners, and it will be hoped that Spain will maintain a neutral position while these hostilities last.

Britain fully understands Spain’s current difficult position, and also appreciates it’s past close ties with both Nazi Germany and Italy, but Britain must do everything in it’s power to protect itself, it’s Commonweath, and it’s overseas interests, especially in the Mediterranean.

With this is mind, His Majesty’s Government feels that joint ownership of the Rock of Gibraltar, together with it’s town, waters and possessions is the best way of preventing it from falling into the hands of it’s enemies. With this in mind, in exchange for Spain’s neutrality in the current hostilities, Britain undertakes to open negotiations with Spain at the cessation of hostilities and to grant them joint ownership of the Rock of Gibraltar for a period of seventy years, whereupon it will then revert to Spanish ownership.”

“Explosive stuff eh Duke? Especially in the wrong hands”, teased the Spaniard.

“Especially for the British Government I would think”, sneered the Duke.

“So when they find that you had been in the room where Juan Galvez Moreno was murdered, and that the document that they badly want back is missing, will they put two and two together?”, was the imposter`s caustic reply.

The Duke of Avila needed time to think. This man had him tied up all ways it would seem, but he had no intention of giving in to blackmail, or betraying his country, or of compromising Britain. A woman’s life may be at stake however, and this creature in front of him wouldn’t have come all this way just to pretend that he was a murderer. He had to play for time.

“Give me your ultimatum, damn you, and tell me who you really are”, he decided.

“My name is unimportant to you at the moment Duke, you will find that out in due course. The arrangement is this. You will give me 1000 pounds in cash, now before I leave this office”.

Avila started to protest,but the other held his hand up as if to tell him that he was wasting his time.

He continued, “You can manage that Duke, you would probably spend that amount in a month on your *vices*. Then, during the course of the next couple of days I will contact you by phone, to give you the details of a foreign bank account to where you will make a transfer of the balance of the 5000 pounds”. Seeing the Duke raise his eyebrows he quickly followed with, “That is right, another 4000 pounds, and when I have proof that the transfer is made you will get the Agreement back".

Instead of the expected outburst, the Duke asked calmly, "And what guarantee do I have that the document will be returned to me?"

"I give you my word Don Carlos, if that isn't too low for you. Anyway, do you think the British would let it go like that? I rather think they would search the world for me don't you?"

"Just where are you thinking of slinking off to", asked the Spanish Representative.

"Again, you don't need to know that until you receive my phone call. Do not try to be clever though Duke and do not contact the police. They will be involved soon enough".

"Let me get this straight, Avila said, sitting down, "If I give you 1000 pounds now, and transfer another 4000 pounds when you call me with the bank account details, you will let the girl go?"

"Of course, replied the other, "and then Galvez Moreno will have his own passport on him, and Arancha will be able to clear your name from any involvement. No one will even have to know about your relationship with her, unless the police decide to broadcast it of course, which I doubt. Then, after a few days you will have the Agreement delivered to you personally by messenger".

"By which time you will be out of the country I presume?"

"We will, replied the blackmailer, "do not forget that there are two of us".

"He must be as sick as you, holding a hostage and a dead body in that apartment. Very well, it seems I have no choice, my safe is in the inner office".

The Duke was told to go ahead, and the other man stood behind him to make sure there were no arms hidden in the safe.

"So, said Avila, "if I call the police now and they catch you in the street........?"

"You know Arancha's apartment has good views of the street, replied the fake envoy, "My friend is waiting for a sign from me, or knows what to do if he doesn't receive one. He can get out of the building very quickly if he has to, but don't worry my Duke, the Agreement is not there. Apart from that, the police will find the body and me with 1000 pounds that you have just given me as a bribe. I'm sure they will put two and two together".

Don Carlos, the Duke of Avila thought long and hard. He had given the imposter the cash he had demanded, but had no intention of transferring one penny more. He would wait an hour then call the police, and then they could trace the phone call when the blackmailer decided to call him. After all, the two criminals had already murdered once, and his life and that of Arancha's would have been in danger too, had he not paid up.

CHAPTER 7

Bill Harris was impatient for news and disliked small talk at a time like this, but said to his assistant with a smile, "So, how are you getting on with our Methodist Minister Tim?"

"Ok, I think, she's a nice girl. Look Sir, I was thinking of inviting her for lunch or for something in the evening. Perhaps in that pub near her chapel. Why don't you come along?".

"Alright Tim, if we are both free I will. Don't want to butt in though!", he laughed.

"Personal phone call for Detective Harris", called out the desk sergeant, "You can take it in the Inspector's office Sir".

"Harris here", he spoke down the phone.

"Hello Bill, it's Ian. Looks like we could have a lead here, and it could be big".

Ian Green was Bill Harris's direct superior in M15 headquarters in London, and it was he who had sent Harris and Cartwright to investigate the killing in Somerset. About middle height and stocky, Ian Green looked the physical type who would be more at home on a rugby field than in an office, but his direct and authoritative manner had got him a long way.

"Go on Sir", Bill said calmly.

"We think your dead man could be the same person who blackmailed the Spanish Ambassador in London a couple of days ago. It seems he murdered an envoy that Franco had sent over here and took his identity. It's rather a long story, but this man and his accomplice intended fleeing the country with money this Ambassador was forced to give them. There's more to it than that, but if your man there is this Juan Pardo, then we have to catch his partner and retrieve something he stole from the real envoy".

"So our man got himself killed in a brawl, and his partner is in a tight spot. But why have we only just been told about this if it happened a couple of days ago?", asked Harris.

"Because it's a very delicate matter at Government level, and quite hush hush", replied Green.

"But you know the whole story Sir?".

"All that I need to Bill, and I am sending a full report of everything that you need to know by messenger. You should have it in a couple of hours. Listen Bill, you and Cartwright are the men on the spot, and I reckon you have about 48 hours to apprehend this fugitive and recover what he, or his partner have stolen", advised Harris's superior.

Bill Harris was thinking, and replied to Green, "If Pardo came down to Somerset it was for a good reason, and I would think it unlikely he would leave this *stolen item* with his friend back in London..."

"And as the missing item wasn't on your man's body, then he may have hidden it somewhere safely until his friend had finished his part of the scheme in London, and rejoined him there. You found flight tickets and money, so I don't need to tell you your job Bill. Forty eight hours remember, or else Scotland Yard will have to take over. The Minister doesn't want that if we can finish the job ourselves", Green warned. "Find that man, and that document".

A top report arrived from London for the M15 men that afternoon, and when Harris had finished reading through it he was on the phone to Inspector Green again, who received the call on a scrambler.

"Well you know as much as I do now Bill", he started.

"Tell me more about the entry and search of the flat Sir", requested Detective Harris.

"The Duke isn't really a full blown Ambassador, Spain doesn't have one here yet, but he is

Franco's man. He waited just over an hour after the imposter had left his office with the money he had handed over to him, then cleverly called an unnamed friend of his, one who knew how to contact ourselves rather than the police. One of our men stayed with the Duke in his office, while myself and Tom Jennings went to the apartment".

"Armed I hope?", asked Harris.

Green ignored the question but just said, "Better make sure *you* are".

"Anyway, he continued, "they had to force their way into the Spanish woman's apartment, and there was no one there. They found chloroform and rope, so she had probably been made inactive while they held her hostage".

"And the Spanish envoy, this Galvez Moreno, was his body there?".

"No it wasn't, replied Green, "but they found it on the ground floor where the boilers and meters and stuff are, He had been knifed ok, and the Duke identified the body from photographs as probably the real envoy".

"So where is the girl? The accomplice must have taken her with him, but why?", asked Harris.

"We don't know that yet, but it's probably because he hasn't heard from his friend yet and is panicking. That is another reason for stepping stealthly, her life is obviously in danger".

"Tell me Sir, went on Harris, "were any of the girl's belongings missing, do you know?.

"We think certain *essentials* were taken yes, but funnily enough not her passport, it was in a drawer. Authentic too, in the name of Arancha Gomez Ruiz".

"Tell me this Sir, he went on, "were there any suitcases in the apartment?"

"No Bill, there weren't any", replied Green.

They both hung up. "Hmmmmm, thought Harris," I wonder".

He filled Cartwright in on this new information, and his partner said, "There goes our lunch date with Marjorie then!"

"On the contrary, replied Harris, "I want us to speak with her more than ever".

Tim was puzzled, but said nothing except that he would make the date for tomorrow lunchtime in The Post Inn.

"In the meantime, we have some thinking to do Tim", said the senior M15 man.

"This person won't know about his accomplice's murder, but he will know that he hasn't been contacted, so in all probability will come here to find out what has happened".

"Especially as our dead man had the flight reservations and cash", put it Tim.

"Exactly, said his boss, "but he will be treading carefully, and even more so when he finds out about the murder. Tim, we are going to put details in the London papers, stating that an unknown man of presumed foreign nationality has been found dead on the railway lines of a sleepy Somerset village. That will almost certainly bring him here, and it will be interesting to see what he does".

"Ok, that's fine, said Cartwright, "and he shouldn't be too hard to spot and arrest".

"Not straight away though, replied his boss, "don't forget that we have to retrieve that document, whatever it may be. I have been told that it is of vital importance, and that our main aim is to get it back. If we arrest him straight away then he could deny all knowledge of its whereabouts, but on the other hand, if we keep him under observation he may know where if it is hidden, and lead us to it".

"Hmmm, might be difficult", said Cartwright dismally.

"Maybe, replied Harris, "but I have an idea".

CHAPTER 8

A report was duly placed in the London and national newspapers the next day, but with the added information that a funeral service would be held at the Hollow Down Chapel for the unknown man, followed by internment at the Stanten cemetery.

Harris and Cartwright were enjoying a typical ploughmans lunch with Marjorie Knight the Methodist Minister. She had agreed to help the two M15 men it what they assured her was a matter of national importance, and Tim Cartwright's good looks could have had something to do with swaying her normal good judgement! She had taken immediately to the young detective, but Harris frightened her a little with his serious bearing.

"So we think this person may come to see you to ask about the funeral Marjorie. He won't be a danger, not to you anyway, but Tim will be in hiding in the chapel ", said Bill Harris gravely.

"And I just tell him the bare details I know, and listen carefully to what he asks me?" replied the Minister.

"Exactly. Now, I have an idea who this person is, but I can't share that at the moment, not even with Tim, but whoever it is, I am gambling that the person won't be too pleased that his partner is being given a non-Catholic funeral", Harris went on.

"Then why isn't he, asked Marjorie, "He is Spanish or Italian isn't he?"

Cartwright chipped in, "Yes he's Spanish Marjorie, and he is being given a proper Catholic funeral service by our friends in Downbury. This is a ploy to try to get him to show himself".

"That's right, confirmed Harris, "and now I want to arrange a meeting between the three of us, together with the Cof E vicar from Stanten, and the Abbott of Downbury!"

"Wow, said the Methodist Minister, "that will be an experience. Do you think they will allow me on their territory?", she laughed. "And what should I wear? I've never been to an Abbey before".

"I guess we will have to be on our best behaviour, said Cartwright warming to the theme, "It could be a little heavy going!"

"Well, said Harris, "I must make the arrangements for this meeting, so you too had better make your own for our expected guest".

With that, the senior M15 man instructed the police radio car to take him to Stanten, where his first call would be to see the Vicar of that parish.

After looking around the small Methodist chapel at Hollow Down, Tim decided that he would make himself at home in the vestry/come changing room. A campbed was procured, and Marjorie would sneak meals in for him, as it was important that someone was there all the time for the next few days. Cartwright felt inside his jacket for the bulk of his Mauser 08, something that Marjorie should never know about, or would ever have allowed inside the chapel, but they were dealing with desperate individuals who had already killed.

Senior Detective William Harris was thirty eight now, married with a two year old daughter, and lived in London. Bill had joined the Metropolitan Police at age eighteen, and after nine years on the beat joined the CID. He had shown great promise, and looked set for a brilliant career as one of the force's brightest young detectives. That was before the war started two years later however. Harris quickly made sergeant in his infantary battalion, and was slightly wounded in the Dunkirk landings. Making it back to the UK safely, Harris was put forward for promotion, was a full lieutenant within a year, and attached to Intelligence. After full training, Harris made one parachute jump with his unit into occupied France in 1943. Although a success, the operation was the last that he would make as it was thought that, at thirty three years old, he could best serve the allied cause in planning future raids etc. He finished the war in destinction as Captain, and belately married Catherine, who was one of his junior officers in 1945, Laura being born a year later.

Catherine probably knew what sort of life she and her future children would have living with husband, after seeing him eased from the post war police into the secret realms of Britain's M15. She didn't know much about his work of course, and didn't ask more than she knew she should.They were both still quite young, and were privileged in regard to many other people who were struggling in the post war years. London gave her too many bad memories though, and one day she would love to move back to her beloved Dorset.

Harris wasn't a religious person in the sense that he attended church regularly, but like the majority of Britons would regard himself a Christian, and was baptized in the Anglican faith. Also like many, he was rather in awe of the Roman Catholics, and wasn't really looking forward to the meeting he was about to arrange.

Driving through the rural landscape, Harris appreciated how people were proud of their birthplace. The villages and hamlets of Somerset nestled in and around the Mendip Hills, and many of them were only approachable through narrow country lanes. This time of year when the foliage was full the hedgerows made driving visibility very bad, and woe betide if you met a farmer coming the other way on his tractor. He wondered what the Yanks must have thought of English country lanes when they were here for the build up to D Day, and what it must have been like trying to drive tanks and trucks through them. When they got to France though, the hedgerows of Normandy had held much greater dangers for them and their allies.

The country air was clean and bright, although when they got closer to the village several gardens had bonfires going in their vegetable plots. Called couch fires locally, they would burn for days, or even weeks if attended properly. Gardeners would hack off the surface of the weeds, and when their fire was going well would place the turves face down all around it, replacing them with more when they had burned through. An opening was made in the side facing the wind for draught, and when the fire was finally out the ashes were excellent fertiliser for their vegetable garden.

Approaching the war memorial in the middle of the village, the driver stopped to ask a local the way to the church.

"Lost be ee, me cock?, asked the villager, "just go on down this lane a bit, baint far, on thee left".

"Well?", Harris asked the driver.

"I think he said it's down here on the left Sir". They both smiled.

The Vicar lived in a quite modern detached house with large lawns and flower beds, and this residence was right next door to the parish church. The church itself was a splendid Norman construction from the 15th Century, and it shared its Saints name with only one other in the British Isles.

Reverend Phillips was a tall, thin man in his late fifties, with a rather academic and retiring air. Bill Harris still towered over the vicar though as he greeted the M15 man, and formally offered him a cup of tea which Harris politely refused, asking for a cold drink instead.

"You have lovely gardens here Vicar, commented the detective, "it seems the whole village has"

"Yes Mr Harris that's true. And most of the gardeners are in a hurry before the 25th of April".

Harris looked puzzled, so the Vicar continued, "It's a local tradition you see, the men must have their runner beans planted before that date".

The London man nodded soberly, only thinking previously that his greens came from the local greengrocers!

"Well, Mr Harris, he changed the conversation, "how can I be of assistance? You mentioned briefly on the phone something about arranging an interrment here for an unknown foreign gentleman who had died locally? Of course, if this is confidential government business then I must consult with the Bishop, but isn't this rather unusual, and doesn't the man have any relations. Is he even of our faith?"

Bill Harris held up his hand as if to say "Whoa, slow down Vicar, one question at a time".
"Telling your Bishop is one thing I don't want you to do Reverend Phillips, at least not yet, and when I say I, that of course means *the powers that be*. I am going to take you into my confidence as much as I can at the moment Sir, Harris continued, "and I hope it doesn't shock you too much when I tell you that this man died under strange circumstances and , that I am 99% sure that he is not of your faith. As an Anglican that is".

"Good gracious, exclaimed the Churchman, " but I can't authorise a burial myself under these circumstances".

"You won't need to, went on the agent, "we just want this man's accomplice to think that his partner is to have a funeral service and burial here. We need this person to show himself, and this is a ruse. Hopefully his curiosity, and possibly his anger at the choice of funeral will bring him out in the open".

The Vicar looked suitably bewildered, and Harris waited for him to speak.

"So is he a Christian?", he asked.

"A Roman Catholic, we think", replied Harris quickly.

"Ah, ah, muttered the Vicar, "I see, I see. Then why not.........?"

"Why not let them handle the funeral? I thought I had explained that Sir but listen, said Harris, "We need your help in this ruse, that's all, but we also need you to please attend a meeting where I will try to explain everything I can to you all".

"To us all, meaning who Mr Harris?, asked the Vicar, "who is to attend this meeting?"

Harris looked amused and said, "Apart from the two of us, possibly my assistant Detective Cartwright, the Methodist Minister from the local chapel, and the Abbot of Downbury!"

Harris thought the Vicar was going to throw him out of his house, but although he turned rather pale just said, "I see, well who would have thought it".

Harris could see that the Vicar was struggling with his emotions, and put in,"It is nothing to worry about Reverend, and no one will be compromised, you have my word".

"And where will this *meeting* be held Mr Harris?", asked Reverend Phillips.

"Well I'm afraid it may have to be at Downbury Sir", replied the other.

"Of course, of course, exclaimed the Reverend, "have to play away from home sometimes I suppose, what?" he uttered cheerlessly.

CHAPTER 9

The idea was that Marjorie would be in the chapel attending to her normal day to day duties as Minister, while Cartwright would be secreted away in the vestry should anyone call. Destiny was about to intervene though, and Marjorie called in to see Tim with bad news.

"Tim, she said, looking distraught, "Mrs Dimmock has sent a message to say that her husband has taken a turn for the worse, the doctor has been called but they don't think he will last the day. I 'm sorry but I must go to them".

"Of course you must, said the young Agent sympathetically, "I can manage here, maybe no one will come anyway".

"What will you do if someone does call?", Marjorie asked in earnest.

"I will have to pretend that I am the Minister I suppose, he laughed, "will it matter if I am in civvies?"

"No, not at all, answered the young Minister, "after all you won't be holding any services or doing any preaching, and I will be back later this evening".

"That's true, well I shall just have to bluff my way through if necessary", he finished.

The day passed quietly, then at around three in the afternoon Cartwright heard a light knock on the door followed by someone calling his name softly. He recognized it straight away as that of his boss, and went to let Harris in.

"All quiet Tim?, he asked", I was told the news about Ken Dimmock, he has died you know, Marjorie will be back later".

"Poor man, replied Cartwright, "he must have suffered a lot".

"This may sound callous Tim, said Harris, but what has happened may help us".

"Sir?", inquired his assistant.

"Ken will have to have a funeral service here in this chapel, and as far as I know he will be buried in the village cemetery. Now, if our stranger comes around asking, or looking, for information about his friend's funeral, then perhaps we can confuse him, or at least it may increase the chances of him showing himself", said Harris thoughtfully.

"Could we perhaps, make a *small change* in the name in the death register here Sir".

"Hmmm, possibly, but of course if our man attends the actual service then he will know the truth. I have some more news Tim", he said more brightly.

"How did the visit go with the Vicar then Sir?", asked Cartwright.

Harris laughed and said, "Well I think he was dreading having to go to Downbury to meet with the Abbott, poor man".

"Marjorie too, sniggered Tim, I think she is wondering what she should wear, but I told her that she's not going to see the Pope himself!"

"But you said that the Vicar *was* dreading a visit to the abbey Sir", went on Cartwright.

"That's right, replied Bill Harris, "and you can tell Marjorie this too. The Abbott has suggested we have our meeting in the snug of the local pub! Hope she won't mind", he smiled.

"Well what a turnup, replied Tim, "she won't mind at all I'm sure. But the Vicar?"

Bill laughed, and reserved judgement!

"Look Tim, he said getting serious again, "I don't like the idea of us messing with the chapel's register or official documents, but what about if we get something semi official, some kind of temporary form that we can leave out".

"Leave it to me Sir, said Cartwright, "I've got time on my hands and can make up some sort of pending funeral service form, something that will give the barest of details, but will look as though it will be inserted in the chapel register in full later on".

"Good, replied his senior, "I'll leave you to it. Good luck, and don't forget that there is a phone at The Post".

"Yes I know, mused Tim, "and I was wondering if that was where our stranger was going in a hurry when he was set upon by those youths. What else would he be doing at that time of night in a quiet place like this, unless he lived here?"

"Good thinking, we'll make a detective of you yet!", grinned Harris before leaving.

That night was sultry and close, the sort where you half expect a thunderstorm to come and clear the air. The horse-chestnut trees that lined the lane seemed heavy and brooding, their spectacular spring colours invisible until the morning. Tim had slept fitfully on and off in his makeshift campbed, but woke up around 1.30 sweating. Unable to go back to sleep, he decided to take some air and have a smoke.

He first had a quick look out the front, but the lane was deadly quiet, a strongish wind was getting up and blowing the clouds along so that the moon shone intermittently. Tim recalled talking to one old man who told him about a storm they had had here in the early nineteen thirties. Unable to sleep that night either, the handful of families who lived in Hollow Down and The Post cowered in their homes hearing trees crashing down one after another. Great trees that had stood for years were destroyed in that terrific storm, and a nearby wood, the name of which the old man told him, but he had forgotten, had all but disappeared by the morning. He felt a shiver go through him, and all of a sudden felt lonely and longed for the crowds and bustle of London. The feeling soon passed however…

Cartwright closed the front door but didn't lock it, then went out the back way. Here it would have been pitch black if there weren`t a moon, and Tim stood on the piece of waste ground that was at the back of the chapel. In daylight it would have looked a bit of an eyesore, and amongst the rubbish thrown there and against the hedge was an old, broken harp. If he had seen it he might have wondered if Methodists had angels, and if one of them had left it's instrument here!

He got his packet of Players out and lit one up, inhaling deeply. He took a second drag, and then thought he heard something. Pricking up his ears, "yes" he thought, it sounded like someone walking on the gravel. Tim quickly threw his cigarette down and quietly put it out with his foot, making for the back door. He couldn't make it though as he heard the gentle opening of the front door, so crouched down under the window sill. It was too dark to see inside, but suddenly a light showed, whoever had found the open door to the chapel had a torch with them, and they wouldn't be expecting anyone to be inside.The M15 man dare not show himself or disturb the intruder,but the maddening thing is that he was caught unawares, and probably wouldn't be able to get a glimpse of whoever it was.

After only about five minutes he could hear the door gently closing again, and stole quietly round to the front of the chapel, cursing himself for having left his pistol inside the vestry. After a cursory look around him, Cartwright walked out to the lane and squinted his eyes to look left and right, but could see nor hear sign of anyone. Turning to go back to the chapel, Tim started as he heard a deep roar getting closer to him. Pushing himself up against the wall of the building he waited, hardly breathing, to see where the noise was coming from. He didn't have long to wait though as an AA motorcycle combination passed him by! Tim remembered seeing an Automobile Association phonebox down on the main Bath to Shepton Mallet road, just over the crossroads and close to The Post Inn.

"What is he doing out this late?", Tim thought to himself. It seemed unlikely that anyone except a genuine AA man would be riding this powerful bike, but at least he had an advantage over the man, who obviously was unaware that he had been seen by the Government official. Interviewing him tomorrow could be interesting….

The rest of the night passed without incident, and Cartwright was able to report to his senior the fact that the late night intruder had read his forged register insert.

What Cartwright had actually written was that the rests of the unknown male found dead in this parish would be interred in the Anglican cemetery in Stanten, and that as his denomination was unknown, a graveside service would be held for him. This he hoped would deter the man's accomplice from attending Ken Dimmock's bona fida funeral here in the chapel, but that he may be enticed to attend the burial thinking that it was for the Spaniard. Several undercover men would be watching out for likely strangers, and if there were any, their following behaviour and movements would be closely scrutinized.

When told of the AA patrolman the next morning, Detective Harris immediately got Bath Police to check out on who he could be, and to arrange for him to be taken to the local Radstock station where he would be interviewed by the detective himself.

"So you had quite a scary night eh Tim?, he smiled. "but we have made some progress".

"Well I'd never really felt so lonely as I did last night Sir, replied Cartwright,"then, when I saw that AA chap roaring along with the moon shining on him, I thought of poor old Ken's visions of the Roman Chariot that he say haunts the area!"

They both laughed a little uneasily.

CHAPTER 10

By midday Patrolman Eric Reed had been identified as the one Cartwright had probably seen the night before. His wife told the constable who called, that Eric had worked late and was still sleeping, so she was asked to tell him to report to Radstock station by 3pm in relation to one of their investigations.

It turned out that Reed was on night duty call-out, and that he had attended a driver who had run out of petrol near Stepton Mallen, after driving back from a meeting and night out in Bath.

"And did you take this man's details Patrolman?", asked Harris.

"Yes Sir, of course, he replied, "it's standard procedure. I have them here in my log".

The book was handed over to the Detective who read out the name of Bill Charlton. His address was in Stepton, and Reed also had all the man's car details logged.

"And was this just a straightforward call out Mr Reed, albeit a late one?", asked Harris unhopefully.

His ears pricked up though when the AA man replied, "Well, this driver seemed very angry. Not just because he had run out of fuel I mean, but he seemed to be angry about someone causing his problem".

"How do you mean, was there someone with him?", pried Harris.

"He was on his own, but he said something about someone had let him down, and had given him the runaround", explained Reed.

"And you didn't ask him what he meant?", went on Harris.

"Well Sir, he had obviously been drinking, and I was encouraging him to get home and off the road as soon as possible". Reed pondered, and then added, "If you have to see this man, I hope I haven't got him into any trouble Mr Harris".

"Not at all, he replied, "I'm not interested in his drinking and driving, unless he had an accident of course", Harris added with some irony.

"And tell, asked the Agent, "why exactly were you riding down Hollow Lane after you had been to your call. You don't live around there do you?"

"Well as you know Mr Harris, there is one of our phone boxes down on the main road, and I had to call in to report. It's standard procedure".

"Of course, replied Harris, not knowing if it was or not. "And you never saw anyone else at all in the vicinity of the chapel, say?" The Patrolman answered in the negative, and was dismissed for the time being.

A constable was sent to the house of Bill Charlton, and as he seemed reluctant to talk in front of his wife, she was told that it was over some trouble in Bath, and that the police were just looking for witnesses. In the circumstances, the constable told him to present himself at Stepton Police Station.

Tim Cartwright had arranged for Bill Harris and himself to eat with Marjorie Knight, the Methodist Minister that night in The Post Inn, and the landlord served up the best fare he could in these difficult times of rationing.

After their meal, coffee was served. Marjorie said she didn't mind the two men smoking, but declined one herself saying, "Nothing to do with my calling, she laughed, "I just never started to smoke. I have never even tried one".

"Well don't start now Marjorie, said Bill, "Tim and I have had a misspent youth".

"I will have that brandy now though, she replied, "you see I'm not all that innocent!"

Harris ordered three brandies, and while they were waiting for them he said, "Are you ok about tomorrow's meeting Marjorie?"

"Well, she replied, "I can't help feeling that the Abbott will be meeting us in the Coach Arms to accommodate me. I mean, maybe women aren't allowed in the abbey?"

"Possibly, in certain parts of it I suppose, replied the agent, "but I expect the Vicar is feeling the same trepidation as you".

Cartwright took a sip of his brandy that had just arrived, and it seemed to loosen his tongue a little as he said, "It will be a bit like being around Germans and trying not to mention the war".

"How do you mean?", asked the minister.

"Well, we shall have to be careful not to mention Henry VIII and all that, won't we?"

They all three laughed.

Harris then brought up the events of the night before, and asked Tim, "So you heard nothing after your visitor left. No car engines?".

"No, it was as still as the grave", he said. Then looked at Marjorie and apologised for his remark.

She hadn't minded though, and Bill asked her about Ken Dimmock.

"He slipped away peacefully in the end, he had been heavily sedated of course", she remarked.

"So you didn't get to speak to him?", inquired Harris.

"Oh no, she replied, "but the last time he was coherent, he told his wife that he had stopped seeing the Roman chariot!"

"Good for him, put in Cartwright, "that probably means that he was in peace".

They all finished their drinks thoughtfully, and Harris asked for the bill. Marjorie wanted to pay her share but was deterred. "Tim and I will put it to costs, and thank you for a delightful evening Marjorie. We will pick you up tomorrow lunchtime".

He then left her and Tim alone for a while to say their goodnights.

There was no need for Cartwright to stay hidden in the chapel that night, so the two detectives motored back to Bath, and before going to their lodgings, called into the police station to check on the interview with Charlton.

Harris read the interview report in silence, then said to the desk sergeant, "It says here that he had a passenger who he had picked up in Bath and who had wanted a lift out this way, but he would prefer not to mention the incident, and that anyway he hadn't asked the person's name. "Who the hell interviewed him?" he shouted.

"An Inspector Hall it says there Sir, I don't know him personally", replied the sergeant glibly.

"Well I bloody well want to Sergeant, get Stepton on the phone, and if Hall isn't there, find out where I can speak to him", ordered the M15 man.

"Yes Sir, replied the sergeant, colouring,"right away".

After about ten minutes Hall had been located, and he answered the phone.

"Who am I speaking to?", he demanded.

"You are Hall?",inquired Harris.

"Inspector Hall yes, and who may you be?", he asked in a broad West Country accent.

"My name is Harris, I am from Government Security in London, and you will address me as Sir. Is that understood Hall?".

A pause from the other end, then "Yes Sir,,they didn't tell me".

"It seems most people are reluctant to tell in your town Inspector", Harris remarked acidly.

"Sir?" inquired the other.

"About this statement you took from William Charlton last night. Why wasn't he made to give you information about the passenger he took out with him from Bath?"

"Made to Sir?, replied Hall airily, "Mr Charlton is hardly a man to be made to do anything, he is the chairman of the Town Council here you know, and quite an influential man. He hadn't broken any laws except maybe having a little too much to drink, and for reasons best known to himself didn't want to expand on his explanations. In fact Sir, he was bloody angry at being dragged into the police station like a common criminal as he put it, and well Sir, I am in the dark as to what all this is about".

Harris thought the Inspector had a point there, and admitted to himself that he was bloody angry too at not being told all the facts of the case he was being ordered to investigate.

"Alright Inspector. I shall come up myself tomorrow afternoon and will see our Mr Charlton in private. It is important as you can now guess, otherwise I wouldn't be here".

Harris's prickly interview with the rural Inspector had put him in a bad mood, and after doing some thinking, decided to give his direct superior in London a call.

Ian Green was glad to hear from him, but slightly wondered why his man in the field had called him outside of their usual agreed times.

"Hello Bill, glad we have a probable suspect down there, can we talk normally?"

"Of course Sir, replied Harris, it's a general type of conversation I want to have with you, but something I must sort out now."

"Fire away detective!", Green replied good naturedly.

"Look Ian, said Harris, unusually addressing his fellow, but superior Inspector, "I really need to know what this case is all about. The document we have to retrieve is all important, but I have come to the point where I need to know what it is, and what the implications of it not being found are. In short, you need to have confidence in me to do my job properly".

There was a longish pause on the other end, then Green replied, "I would have said the same thing in your place Bill, but it isn't my decision you understand".

"I know that, but if I don't know the whole story my hands may be tied".

"Personally Bill, I wonder you haven't asked me this before, and it is to your credit that you have waited so long. I will speak to *upstairs* today, and you can rest assured that I will be 100% behind your request", said Green placatingly.

CHAPTER 11

Harris and Cartwright picked up Marjorie the next day in their commandeered car, and pulling into the carpark of the Coach Arms, were surprised to see the Vicar standing there. "Hello Vicar, said Harris cheerfully, "sorry we are a little late, but why didn't you wait inside?"

It was quite a cold morning, and a very light drizzle was falling.

"Oh no, it's quite alright, replied Reverend Phillips, "I have only just arrived myself, and thought I heard your car coming".

Cartwright gave a tight grin, and then took it on himself to introduce Marjorie.

"Vicar, do you know Miss Knight? She is from the chapel".

"Never met before, replied the churchman, "but heard of you of course. Hello my dear", he half bowed rather stiffly.

"Blimey, thought Tim, "if *he* doesn't approve of female ministers, what will the Abbott think!"

Their fears were unfounded however, for when the four entered the warm interior of The Coach Arms in South Street it was to find the Abbott stood up to the bar talking with the landlord, a half pint of real ale in front of him, and a cigarette in his hand!

He turned to greet them, a kindly, horn-rimmed spectacled man in his late sixties, who looked more like an academic than a religious. He was in fact both.

Bill Harris stepped forward and introduced himself first, then Marjorie. "Abbot this is Miss Marjorie Knight, and she is the Methodist Minister of Hollow Down".

The Abbott took her offered hand warmly and said, "It's a pleasure my dear, and as we introduce each other I will ask you what you would like to drink".

"No Sir, that's quite alright, I will see to them", cut in Harris.

"Nonsense, replied the other, "what will it be my dear?".

Marjorie said she would have a shandy.

The Vicar was introduced next, and Rev Phillips looking and feeling uncomfortable, asked for an orange juice. Harris and Cartwright gave each other a quick look as if to say,"No wonder he didn't want to come into the pub on his own!"

Finally Tim Cartwright was introduced, and the two MI5 detectives asked for a pint of real ale, being assured by the Abbot that it was excellent.

The Arms, as the name suggested, was an old coaching inn, and still had a ring on the outside wall where horses used to be tied up. It was small and dimly lit inside, but cosy and warm.

"Michael, the priest called to the landlord,"a small shandy, an orange juice and two pints of your best ale. You had better fill my half up as well. Mr Harris, shall we have them served in the Snug Bar? It's more private there, although at this time of day Michael usually only gets a few locals in".

It was agreed to be a good idea, and the landlord brought their drinks into the small, inner room that had a nice fire going for this chilly lunchtime.

Michael the landlord was a stout man in his early fifties, and his ruddy face and long side whiskers made him look like someone out of a Dickins novel. "No, you won't be disturbed here, he said, "I expect old Gaffer Oswald will be in shortly, but he thinks that chair in front of the bar fireplace is his own. He's seen about 10 landlords come and go here in his lifetime!"

They all chuckled at this, then after Harris had wriggled his six feet three frame into a chair, spoke first.

"Well thank you all three for agreeing to this meeting. Each of you knows something of what myself and Detective Cartwright are investigating in your parishes, and I hope to fill in some of what you don't know. I want to ask all three of you for your assistance in this matter, which I can assure you is of vital national importance, so I won't need to stress the need for total secrecy about what we will discuss here in this room", Harris looked around him for effect, and also to satisfy himself that no one else was listening in. "All three of you have a special place in this village and surrounding areas, and I sincerely hope that you can use your influences to ward off any questions or rumours that may be circulating, he continued, "Tim, would you like to give our guests an update?"

Cartwright looked around at his seated audience, and, catching Marjorie's eye, gave her a quick smile.

"Miss Knight and the Abbot here are aware that the body of a foreign man was found on the railway lines near Hollow Down, and that our investigations have shown that he was murdered. Reverend Phillips gave a short gasp, and Cartwight continued, "I am afraid you know less that anyone at the moment Vicar, but we hope to put you all in the picture now. You may wonder why two Secret Service personnel have been sent down here, even if the deceased person was not British, and taking into account that the war hasn't been over many years. The reason is that this person was travelling on a false passport, and we believe that while in London, he and an accomplice murdered a Spanish envoy who had been sent there by none other than General Franco, and that this murdered envoy's indentity was assumed to trick and blackmail the Spanish representative in London".

"Do you mean the Spanish Ambassador?", asked the vicar, seemingly pleased to be the first of the three ministers to speak.

"I don't believe Spain has an ambassador as such yet reverend", put in the Abbot.

"Quite right, said Bill Harris, "These are very tense times for Franco and his regime, and they need the help of the Allies more than ever now. Not only financially, but protection against the increasing threat of Communism".

"But why did this imposter come down to Somerset, and what is the link with this area?, asked Rev Phillips.

Cartwright took up his story again, "The envoy who was sent from Spain stopped off at Downbury Abbey before going to London. Isn't that so Sir?", he said, looking at the Abbot.

Before replying, Harris asked if anyone had objections to smoking. Marjorie and the Vicar didn't smoke, but had no objections to the others doing so. Harris started to fill his pipe, and Cartwright offered the Abbot one of his cigarettes, who took a long drag on it before saying,

"Yes, this person visited us, and we discussed the possibility of Franco's young successor spending part of his education here. The school has a history of accepting foreign pupils of course, and I personally have somewhat of a connection with Spain. My Mother was Spanish, and I spent part of my childhood in Spain".

"And he had planned to call on you again before going back to Spain Sir?", Cartwright asked the Catholic priest.

"Yes he did, poor man".

Bill Harris could see that the best way to answer the questions that were obviously going to come their way was to go ahead with their story, so he took over.

"The main thing now is that this imposter stole a document from the Spanish envoy, a very important document in the opinion of His Majesty's Government, and we think he brought it with him here to Somerset. Our guess is that he looked similar to the bona fide envoy, and was planning on taking his identity, in yet another disguise. He was found killed here, and we know he has an accomplice in London, probably someone who has lived there for some time".

"A kind of sleeper?", asked Reverend Phillips.

"Yes, possibly", he replied. And we are pretty sure that this accomplice will come here, as we have put the news of an unknown person's death here in the London papers. This other person will almost certainly know, or want to know, where the stolen document is, and we feel that he may lead us to it. In fact, we are almost certain that he is here already, and this is where Miss Knight has been helping us".

Marjorie coloured slightly, and spoke for the first time, "Very little help I'm afraid Mr Harris, but I appreciate that to put your plan into operation it is important that we all three of us know as much as each other".

"Presumably the plan being, put in the Vicar, "to dupe this person into thinking that a forthcoming interment in my cemetery is to be that of his friend?"

"We think it worth a chance reverend, and we hope to… well… annoy this person, as his friend will almost certainly be a Roman Catholic, said Harris looking at the Abbot and adding, "but don't worry, as he will have a real funeral befitting his own faith".

The Abbot nodded at this, and then asked, "But was this imposter's murder anything to do with his criminal activities?"

"We think not Sir, replied the MI5 Detective, he was accidently killed by some drunken youths after he was approached by them. He retaliated by brandishing a knife".

After the explanations were over, Harris was happy that he had given the three church people just enough information to keep them on his side, and that they would keep what they knew to themselves. They then ordered another drink and Harris said to Reverend Phillips, "I believe you were a chaplain in the war Sir?" The vicar put down his soft drink and replied, "Yes Mr Harris, indeed. I went over to France a few days after the Normandy landings, and then stayed with our troops through to Germany. Of course, he added as an adjoiner, "there were Roman Catholic priests there too, we got on very well together". He and the Abbot smiled at each other, and Harris felt that the ice had been broken.

It was Marjorie who then addressed the Abbot, "You mentioned Abbot that you had connections with Spain. I rather think you have also had an interesting past!".

The Abbot stubbed out his cigarette and said smilingly, "Thank you Miss Knight for charming us old men! Although I didn't go myself, our community certainly did have padres attached to the British Army, as Reverend Phillips rightly remarked. In fact, he added humbly, "I went to Spain in 1936 and spent two years of the Spanish Civil War as a padre. Not attached to The International Brigades however".

The Vicar spread out his hands as if to say "It doesn't matter, that was your business".

The Abbot continued, "It will probably answer your question Miss Knight if I explain that my mother was actually Spanish. She was from Extremadura in the South West of Spain, and my father met her when he was a diplomat over there. I was sent here to England to be educated, and then entered theological college. My parents also came back to the UK when the troubles started with the Republic, you know, the burning of churches, killing of priests and nuns etc."

Harris put in, "The war that all this led up to was a very cruel one".

"Terrible, replied the priest, "and there were abominable atrocities on both sides, even before the actual war started, or the Coup, or the Great Crusade, or whatever you prefer to call it. Because of my faith and my background I was attached to Franco's Nationalist forces, and saw much bravery and cruelty on both sides".

The meeting broke up on an agreeable note, and Harris called his assistant aside. "Tim, he confided, "I'm going up to London this evening, but will be back tomorrow. I would have liked to have interviewed our Mr Charlton, but you will have to do it. Forget his standing in the town, we want the truth from him".

"Leave it to me Sir, replied Cartwright, "but can I ask why you are going?".

"I have a meeting with Ian Green. I more or less demanded it Tim, I'm damned if I am to carry on leading these investigations without knowing the truth of the matter".

CHAPTER 12

Bill Charlton burst into the interview room at Stepton police station with a look on his face that would cower lesser men than Tim Cartwright. William Charlton was both the mayor of the town and one of its leading businessmen. He was also a big man physically with a loud voice, and the first thing he bellowed was, "Where is Detective Harris, have I been pulled away from my work to be questioned by his bloody assistant?"

"Sit down please Mr Charlton, said the junior detective, "my name is Cartwright, and I apologise that Detective Harris has had to go to London today".

"To visit the bloody King I suppose?", he boomed.

"Well, let's just say that you are a lucky man that Detective Harris is not here Sir, you wouldn't find him as… friendly as I am".

"Friendly my ass, replied the big man, "I have enough friends in high places, including the Chief Constable of this county, so if you don't get this business over soon and let me get back to mine, he will hear about it..."

Tim Cartwright went red in the face at this, and exploded.

"Ok Fatso I've had enough of your bullshit, now tell me about the person you gave a lift to out of Bath", shouted the detective.

Charlton was first shocked, then crazy with rage to be spoken to like this. "Who the hell do you think you are talking to, you cheeky young devil", he stormed, getting up out of his chair.

Tim quickly pushed him back down though, and the older man looked at him in astonishment.

"Now listen to me Mr Charlton, I don't care who you are or who you know, I am investigating a possible murder, and if you don`t stop threatening me and start to cooperate, you will be in serious trouble", said Cartwright.

"Who the bloody hell are you?", asked Charlton, but in a more respectful tone.

Detective Cartwright slipped his Mauser from beneath his jacket, and laid it gently on the desk in front of Bill Charlton. "I am from MI5 Mr Charlton. Now, shall we start again?"

Charlton nodded his assent but seemed to be hypnotised! Tim quickly pocketed his arm, and asked for some coffee to be brought in. "That's better, he remarked, "some people bring out the worst in me!"

Mayor Charlton was like a lamb now, but still being coy about his passenger.

"Now Mr Charlton, you went to a meeting in Bath and had quite a lot to drink. Ok, I'm not worried about that. Someone approached you and asked if you were able to give him a lift".

"Yes, that's right", he replied.

"But how did he know that you were going south, out into the countryside?"

"Well I'm not sure, but I am quite well known and she could have asked someone".

Cartwright's ears pricked up, "Did you say *she*?"

"Yes, it was a woman, I thought you knew that. I wouldn`t have bloody well given a man a lift at that time of night", he said with some of his old bravado.

"What did she ask you exactly?"

"I told her I was going to Stepton and she said that was fine, but would I stop around Hollow Down on the way as she wanted to get her bearings for a future meeting there with someone", answered Charlton.

"And you agreed. Why?", asked the detective a little incredulously.

"Well, I'd rather not say young man", he replied.

"Come on Sir, we are both adults, and we don't want that AA patrolman to give evidence that you were drunk while driving now, do we?"

"That bugger?, exclaimed Charlton, "If you must know, she called me closer and whispered something in my ear".

"To convince you?".

"Yes".

"And that was?"

Charlton's face started to redden, "I am a married man Mr Cartwright, I don't want this to get out".

"We will do everything we can to protect your name Sir, *if* you are honest with us".

"She said, she said....I'm not wearing any knickers!"

Tim smiled to himself, "So you thought you were on a promise eh Sir? Was she worth it?"

"She was a gorgeous looking woman detective, sort of foreign looking, but she spoke perfect English. A bitch though, as it turned out", Charlton almost spat the words.

"So you didn't make out presumably?", asked Cartwright.

"No, she was obviously using me. Led me on a goose chase round the countryside, ran me low on petrol and then disappeared when I had to call that bloody AA man".

"What didn't you like about him?", asked Tim puzzled.

"He seemed to be distracted and offhand and....".

"Yes?", prompted Cartwright.

"I've got the feeling, I don't know mind, but I've got the feeling that he picked this woman up himself afterwards".

Cartwright put through a call to HQ in London, and was able to speak with his superior just before he was off to catch his Bath train. "I've spoken to this Charlton man Sir, and guess what? The person he gave a lift to was a woman".

"Thanks Tim, but I think I knew that all along. Look, I have to rush, see you in a few hours time".

The MI5 man put down his receiver and swore to himself ", Well I'll be buggered".

CHAPTER 13

Arancha Gomez Ruiz had been fortunate so far. After fleeing London she had managed to get out here to Somerset, and had done well to use the two men she had encountered. One had given her the lift and time to look around, and the other a place to stay the night. Too bad one was an idiot, and the other a pervert. God, she thought, "are all men like this, or do I make them so?". She was thinking back to her relationship with the Count in London who at least had money, and he had proved useful in replacing her passport when she had lied to him about it being lost or stolen.

Now, Arancha had to use all her considerable skill and charm to try to find out what really happened to Pardo, and what he did with the precious document. Would going to his funeral and risk showing herself help her search at all? She decided that she must attend, after all she was a Roman Catholic and it was the least thing she could do to attend her partner's interment, even if the British have got it wrong. She finally decided her best action would be to arrive early at the old Norman parish church, and to see who was there and listen in for any gossip.

Sitting on the back pew, the young Spanish woman didn't have to wait long before she heard an old couple in front mention Ken Dimmock's name. "Excuse me, she leaned forward and asked, "what was the poor man's first name? I can never remember".

The husband and wife, delighted to be able to help an apparent stranger replied almost in unison "Ken, dear. It were Ken Dimmock".

Arancha put a black veil over her head and slipped quietly out of the pew, making for the church door. She had been tricked, she realised that now, and this meant that she was being sought out and would have to do some quick thinking.

The pallbearers were walking up the path carrying Ken's coffin and she had to make her move, so edged closer to the door and just managed to slip out before it passed her. Outside the air was cool and damp, and she looked around her to see that except for one or two people hanging around inside the church, all were now following the procession round the back to the cemetery. One of these was the driver of the hearse who was having a smoke under a tree. He looked at the attractive, black clad lady and said, "Are you ok my love?"

Arancha gave him a cute smile and replied that she just felt a little faint and would take a short walk.

Leaving the cemetery gate she saw the hearse parked outside, together with three or four other cars, so walked along the pavement beside them. The second car in the row was a Ford, and she was in luck, looking through the left side passenger window she saw that the key had been left in the ignition! Walking around the car, she opened the driver's door and slid in, pushing the holdall she carried onto the passenger seat. The interior had a slight smell of chicken shit, but the car was quite clean and tidy. Arancha was an intelligent and resourceful woman, and she quickly sussed out the Ford's basic controls, put it into first gear, and drove slowly away and down the lane.

Around a left hand bend was the Vicarage, and then the lane straightened out for fifty yards before coming to a small junction with a sharp turn to the right where the road dropped into a deepish valley. She stopped the car momentarily and saw that she was parked outside of a busy looking farm, so immediately pulled away again and decided to follow the lane rather than turn to the right.

The hedges round the lane were getting progessively thicker and higher, and as she drove Arancha wondered whether she should try to make for Bath and risk getting stopped by the police, or to try and hold up somewhere nearby. "But where?, she thought, "in this place where everyone knows you"

She had only driven a couple of hundred yards when the lane took a sharp left turn, but something caught the girl's eye. As the direction of the road bore off to the left, it looked like another leafy lane or track went straight ahead, and Arancha thought she saw smoke rising in the air some way off.

Changing down to second gear, she looked in her mirror. "Good, she thought, "not a soul in sight", so without stopping, drove straight ahead to find herself going down what was obviously a no through road, as there was only room for one vehicle. Probably used just for tractors, was what she thought, "but maybe there is a farm down here?"

If the hedges were high before, here they were like a jungle, but soon she came to a muddy entrance to a gate that lead into a field. Stopping the car, she got out and looked around her the best she could. Her tight skirt made it a bit difficult, but Arancha climbed up the gate and looked across the field to the north, where she could just see the roof of what looked like a cottage. There was smoke coming out of the chimney so, climbing back into the car, she carried on driving the car slowly down the lane until she could see that it was definitely a no through road. A large gate barred the way ahead that presumably opened onto the drive of some property, although it looked as though it hadn't been opened in years. To her right, Arancha saw a stile leading into the field where the cottage was, and as the lane was a little wider here at this end, there was be just enough room to turn the car around.

Dusk was already beginning to fall, and the sound of rooks squawking was all that broke the silence. Arancha thought it unlikely that anyone would come down the lane now at this time, so she took the decision to risk leaving the car parked here and to explore the cottage. Before climbing the stile she lifted her holdall over first, then automatically checked her handbag to make sure that her ladies pistol was handy. Whether or not she would have to use force or sympathy remained to be seen, but she was dog tired now and desperately needed somewhere to rest and hide out until morning. The holdall carried her bare essentials, but as she wouldn't now be going to Buenos Aries as planned, her wardrobe hardly mattered until she had a clear plan for the future.

Arancha was glad to see there were no cowpats in the field, not only as she didn't want to step in one in the half light, but also as it showed that the area around the cottage was fairly deserted and a farmer was unlikely to show up. With her town shoes slipping on the damp grass, the fugitive started descending the slope and could now clearly see the welcoming cottage with it's chimney smoking merrily. It was a very old stone cottage and seemed to be partly covered with bushes and trees, with the front facing the thick woods beyond. As she approached the right hand side of the house, the well worn path curved and then straightened up to lead to its front entrance. Before the Spanish woman had a chance to knock on the door, she saw the figure of an old woman at the window who had obviously seen her coming a long way off.

Judy Wilson was known affectionately by the locals as *Granny Wilson*, and her lonely dwelling in the woods as *Granny Wilson's Cottage*. In her late seventies, Judy had been a widow for nearly twenty years, and when her only son was killed in the last war her daughter in law and granddaughter decided to leave the cottage which they shared with her and move into the village. Nothing though would persuade *Granny* to leave her beloved home, and although she had regular visitors, the solitude didn't bother her.

This unexpected visitor decided to use her charm on the old woman, partly because she was so weary, and partly because her arrival must seem so surprising.

"Hello, she called out in her perfect, but heavily accented English, "I'm afraid I am in trouble. My car has broken down and I wonder if you could put me up for the night".

Granny Wilson opened up the door to the stranger with a smile, craftily looking around to see that the well-dressed girl was alone. "Come in dear, she said pleasantly, "where were you going?"

Arancha replied vaguely that she was headed in the London direction, but had got lost after attending a funeral nearby, and then her car conked out.

"I will pay you of course, she added, "God I am so tired. Do you live here all alone?" she pried.

"That I do dear, replied Judy, "and you must be hungry. Go and sit by the fire and I will get you something, and then see to your room. It's nothing special mind".

"I'm sure it will be fine", smiled Arancha.

As she sat by the fire hearing the cosy rattle of tea things being prepared, Arancha almost started to nod off, but jumped up with a start when she heard the front door being opened. Quickly grabbing her bag she withdrew the small pistol and made for the door. "Where are you going?", she shouted at Judy's figure that had disappeared into the garden.

Judy turned around to see, with not much surprise, the gun in the woman's hand and shouted back, "No need for that thing my dear, I'm just going to fill the kettle, I have to get it from this here brook you see".

Arancha put the gun away, feeling angry at herself, but kept the old lady in her sight until she came back in the cottage.

"You be in trouble Miss, that's your business and you be still welcome to stay the night. All I ask is that you be gone in the morning".

"I will be yes. Are you sure that no one will be around here before the morning?", she asked with a different edge to her voice now.

Judy assured her again that no one would, and probably not during the day either, but her quick brain was working still. She knew that this girl must be on the run from someone, and possibly that she was a criminal or a fugitive who was armed and dangerous. Tomorrow was Thursday. Bill Breck the gamekeeper from the woods usually left her a rabbit that he would have caught very early in the morning, and had put inside a wooden box down by the brook for her to collect later. He did this most weeks as a kindness, but when he visited Granny Wilson in person his trusted position demanded that he go there emptyhanded. Judy excused herself to wash the dishes in the kitchen, sensing that the foreign stranger wouldn't want to go to bed yet without seeing that she had retired too. Once in the kitchen she quickly found a scrap of paper and wrote a short note *Tell police, woman inside with gun*" then, hiding it up her sleeve called out to Arancha.

"Dear, I always fill me kettle again before I do go to bed, you can watch me if you like".

Arancha came to the front door and told the older woman to go ahead. As Judy bent down over the stream in the darkness, she deftly slipped the scrap of paper from her sleeve and pushed it into the wooden box.

"I've decided to sleep down here by the fire", Arancha said to Judy as she came back in the sitting room.

"Alright me dear, if you like. I'll get you some blankets".

Outside all was still, and an owl was hooting somewhere. Bill Breck was an early riser, usually around 4.30am or so as he liked to patrol the woods for poachers, and to do a little for himself too. He would go back home for breakfast about eight 'o clock, then have a snooze in the chair for an hour before starting work again.

Bill's son Donald was home on leave from the Army, where he was well into his period of conscription. Don was keen to take over his Dad's job in a few years time, and didn't miss an opportunity to go with him on his early morning patrols. "More fun than the Army", he would say, and of course he liked the feel of a shotgun in his hands, especially as he was now a trained soldier used to a more lethal carbine.

The morning was cold and frosty, and no poachers tracks were seen by the father or son. Bill led the way to one of his own well hidden traps, and sure enough, he had a nice big rabbit there for Granny Wilson. The animal would have died instantly the way Bill caught them, and he told Don to go and leave it in Granny's box. "We'll go round lunch time and taste her stew", he laughed.

Bill told his son that he had a couple more traps to check, and then he would make for home. "If you don't catch me up, I will see you at home then", he waved as he made off into the woods again.

Donald could just make out the outline of the cottage in the breaking light, and was surprised to see smoke coming from the chimney this early, not knowing that the fire had been banked up all night. "Granny must be up already, he thought to himself, "She'll be pleased to see me after all these months", so there and then decided to take her the rabbit himself, keeping it hidden just in case.

Knocking lightly on the door, Don pulled himself up to his full six feet, knowing that Granny would be impressed by his soldierly bearing. He wished his hair wasn't cut so short though, there was a dance in the village hall on Saturday night and he wanted to look good for the local girls. Arancha was already up and about, but started when she heard the knocking." *La madre que te pario*", she muttered to herself, and quickly and silently ran up the stairs to Judy's bedroom.

"Who is that, you old witch; she spat, "you told me no one would be around here yet".

Judy's bedroom window overlooked the front door, and she slowly drew the curtian back and exclaimed, "Why it's young Donald the gamekeeper's son. He must be on leave".

"On leave?", asked the other.

"From the Army, replied Granny, "he's doing his national service". Then added with feeling, "For his King and Country!"

Arancha gave her a sideways look, and told her to go down and let him in. "And I will be right behind you with this", she said, brandishing her gun.

Judy opened the front door wide and feigned surprise, "Donald 'tis you, what a surprise you bin and gave me". Then, before the boy could answer she continued with, "Be your father still away then Don, and he got you to do his work for 'un?". She gave him a sly wink, and Donald looked puzzled as he followed her over the threshold.

 Before he could say anything though Arancha came out from behind the door with the gun in her hand and said, "Put that shotgun down on the table, and don't try to be a brave soldier". As she eyed the smart young man she fleetingly thought how handsome he was.

"I will be gone soon but I need your help, both of you, she said, "No one will get hurt if you do nothing silly".

Donald was nearly 20 years old and fit as a fiddle, and Judy could see that he had got over his initial shock and was itching to have a go at this mysterious, but attractive woman. She had the drop on them both however, and neither wanted to endanger the other.

"I brought along a rabbit for you Granny. When I saw the smoke from your chimney I decided to bring it for you instead of...."

"Instead of what?", Arancha asked suspiciously.

Don was thinking on his feet and replied, "Nothing, just that I would have brought it round later in the morning".

"Put it on the table, and don't try to touch that shotgun", warned the woman.

"Can you drive?", this was to Donald.

"Since I was about twelve", he answered.

"Good, replied Arancha, "my car is up at the end of the lane, you can turn it around for me and come for a little drive".

Don and Granny looked at each other, but realised that they must do the woman's bidding for the time being.

"Now, stand over there both of you", she ordered, and they crossed the room.

Arancha broke the breach of the shotgun and shook the two cartridges out on the floor, then picked them up and put them in her bag. She then went and opened the front door, and holding the shotgun by its barrel, flung it into the brook. She had her scant possesssions ready, and told Donald to lead the way to her car, with a warning to Judy of, "Don't do anything silly for a couple of hours old lady, Donald is all mine for now".

Bill Breck meanwhile was mildly surprised that his son hadn't caught him up yet, but decided to go on home for breakfast anyway. Bill's wife was up and already in the kitchen making the first meal of the day for her two men. Irene was glad to have her beloved son home, even if it was only for ten days, and she called out to both of them when she heard the door.

"Only me, Bill shouted, "Don hasn't caught me up yet. I told him to leave a rabbit for Granny Wilson, but he must think he's out on manoeuvres!". They both laughed, but this turned to concern when Don still hadn't shown up 20 minutes later. Bill finished his breakfast, then lighting his pipe said to Irene, "I think I will take a stroll and see where he's got to".

"Oh Bill, his wife replied, "I hope he hasn't been caught in one of those damned traps of yours".

"Rubbish woman, he snapped, "He's not stupid you know, Don is my son!"

The grassy slope leading up to the lane was still showing signs of frost, and as it melted, the surface was slippery for walking on. Arancha walked behind and suddenly said, "Do you know what *Esse Te seis, cinco, cinco, dos* means?"

"What?", replied Donald. "Is that Spanish or something?".

Arancha looked flustered and coloured, "Sorry yes, that is Spanish, forgive me".

"But what did you say?", asked the youngster.

"I asked you if you know what ST6552 means?"

"ST 6.......", he repeated.

"Yes, ST6552. Does it mean anything to you at all?.

Don looked more puzzled still, and replied in the negative. "Why?"

"Oh it doesn't matter, she replied hastily, "just something someone told me".

"Would it be a code or something?", asked the young soldier.

Arancha decided to open up a bit and said, "Well I am looking for something a friend may have left for me, something important, but I think he has hidden it and wants me to find it, but not any one else." She looked at Donald, and couldn't think of a nicer looking travelling companion or hostage! Perhaps there would be a way to get the document handed over to her after all.

The gamekeeper meanwhile had retraced his steps in the woods, and as Granny's cottage came into view could see something white stuck in the door of her wooden box. Walking quickly towards it, his sharp eye saw the discarded shotgun lying in the shallow brook.......

The fugitive and her prisoner had reached the car, and Donald got the engine to turn over first try.

"A nice car", he observed, but Arancha was in a hurry to move and told him to turn the car around. Donald put the car in reverse gear and let the clutch up carelessly. The Ford jerked backwards and Don pulled hard down on the wheel's right side. This caused the car to lurch into the right hedge with a crash as its rear bumper caught in the thick undergrowth.

"Be careful *idiota*", shouted the woman.

Donald apologized, telling her that he wasn't used to the clutch.

"I'll have to free the bumper though", he added, and got out before Arancha could say anything.

She wound the window down and stuck the gun out, but Donald assured her, "Don't worry Miss, I'm not going to run away".

The young Breck bent down to his task, but swiftly picked up a twig and pushed it into the trye valve nearest to him. Luckily there was no valve cap for him to unscrew, and the air started to whistle out of the tyre.

"Bad luck, he shouted out," it's punctured the tyre".

"*Hijo de puta*, you did that on purpose", she screamed.

"Pardon Miss", replied Donald cockily.

Arancha got out of the car and pointed the gun at Donald's head. "Do something with it, and quickly. I am warning you".

Breck opened up the boot of the car with difficulty due to it being pushed up against the hedge, and started to look for a spare wheel and jack. The car was well looked after and all the spares were there, so he commenced changing the wheel as slowly as he dare.

"Does the old woman have to come this way when she goes out?" Arancha asked the youth, idly looking at her nails and leaning on the car.

"Unless she walks through the woods yes, but that's not likely", he replied.

"And no one else was with you *Donaldo*?", she asked, more friendly.

Don quite liked this version of his name, but answered her in the negative.

The wheel changed, Donald let the jack down, tightened up the wheel nuts, and started to pack the tools and punctured wheel back into the boot. He needed to waste more time though, and noticed a petrol can in the boot, which he shook, and found to be full.

"I noticed that the petrol gauge is showing low Miss, he said, "if you plan to drive a long way you need to fill up".

"Not in this town I shan't", she replied gruffly.

"No need to, there is a full can here. Shall I tip it in?".

Arancha gave him a quick look, and snapped, "*Si*, but make it quick boy".

Again, Donald took as long as he could over the job without making it look too suspicious.
At last they were ready to go, and Donald opened the driver's door. He had probably wasted about forty minutes in all. Arancha gave him a bright smile however, and he couldn't help seeing that her tight skirt had ridden up to show a good expanse of her shapely thighs.

"Come on Donaldo let us go, we have lost too much time, she purred, "perhaps you would like to come all the way to London with me?"

Don tried to keep his mind on his driving, and soon had the car turned around and facing up the no through road towards the village. There was only about 100 yards to go to meet the main lane, although it seemed longer than that with the thick high hedges on either side. As Donald turned the last left hand bend, he momentarily thought that a herd of cows were blocking his exit from the no through road, but soon realised that they were a group of men, some in police uniform!

CHAPTER 14

On seeing his unread note and the discarded shotgun belonging to his son, Bill Breck had rushed to the cottage to find Granny Wilson putting on her coat and boots to go out to sound the warning. After a quick explanation of what had happened, the gamekeeper hurried to Hollow Down Hall where his employers had a telephone.

In a line across the road stood two constables, a sergeant and MI5 agents Harris and Cartwright. Up the road towards the village were two parked police radio cars, one which was occupied by its driver and Doctor Buell. As soon as it was safe, the doctor's concern was for the welfare of Judy Wilson, as well as for the hostaged youth.

Donald was smart and quickly read the situation, but so too did his passenger. In a flash Arancha had the Remington Derringer out of her bag. Because of her position in the passenger seat and being right-handed, she put the upper half of her body out the car window and shot straight at the men.

Then, as Donald would recall later, everything seemed to happen at once. One of the agents returned Arancha's fire, Donald himself opened his car door and fell out onto the road, and then a deafening boom filled the air. Arancha's gun only had two shots, but she didn't get the second one off. Donald's father Bill was behind the left hand side hedge with his shotgun, and suddenly Arancha's head exploded into a red mass as the pellets hit her at short range.

"No, you idiot", shouted Harris too late.

A silence seemed to reign for an eternity, and the smell of cordite filled the air. Dr Buell on hearing the shots was already running towards the scene, accompanied by the police driver. Tim Cartwright was the first to react, and rushed over gun in hand, to see if Donald was ok. Bill Harris and the police sergeant approached the car where the girl's upper torso was still hanging out of the window. It was a pathetic sight to see the woman's sleek black hair and slim figure reduced now to those of a lifeless dummy.

Here of all places, in a peaceful English country lane which two world wars hadn't changed, a scene of city style violence reigned. Donald had long since lost his innocence of youth, but suddenly his memories of bird nesting and picking mushrooms and hazelnuts in these fields came back to him. He wouldn't want his children to witness anything like this…

Bill Breck got through a gap in the hedge, and hearing Detective Harris's shout, approached him with the breech of his shotgun now broken. One of the constables, the youngest one, was vomiting in the opposite hedge. Everyone seemed stunned and whitefaced.

"I didn't mean to kill her, stuttered Breck, she had my son, and she had a gun". He could see that Donald was ok.

"This is the boy's father Sir , Sergeant Biggs said to Harris, "he's the gamekeeper on this estate and he gave the alarm. They phoned from the Hall".

Bill Harris turned on him and barked, "He doesn't even interest me Sergeant, get your constable to check he has a permit for that thing and get him out of here".

Biggs was shocked at the agent's attitude, and replied to him with as much restraint as he could, "He was worried for his son Sir, I think you should go easy on him".

"Bollocks Sergeant, I will ask you when I want your opinion", he rounded on the local man.

Sergeant Biggs was an experienced police officer who had also served as an RSM during the war, he was also older that the MI5 man. Shorter than Harris he may have been, but he was built like a barn.

"Look Mr Harris, he said quietly, "we may be down in the sticks here, but we aren't bloody fools. We have been very cooperative with you two detectives up to now and we still don't know what this is all about, so I would ask you to be a little more civil".

Harris was calming down from the shock of losing possibly his only lead in finding the missing document.

"Yes Sergeant, you're quite right. I apologise", he replied humbly.

"That's alright Sir, Biggs replied, "I realise that you must have wanted this person very badly".

"I did sergeant I did, he replied, "but alive".

Tim Cartwright was dispatched to see that Granny Wilson was ok, accompanied by Doctor Buell, and to also get a statement from her. They needn't have worried though, she was cool as a cucumber, and as soon as she knew that Donald was alright, was lucid in her account of all that had gone on since last evening. She had heard the shots of course, but her questions to Cartwright weren't answered with the same honesty that she had used.

An ambulance had arrived meanwhile, and Arancha's body was taken to Bath Police Forensic Dept. Bill Harris and Sergeant Biggs were driven to the local police station together with Don Breck.

Biggs turned round in his seat and said to the youngster sat in the back, "This will be something to tell the other squadies eh Donald?"

"She was a gorgeous looking woman sergeant. What was she running away from?" When no answer was forthcoming he continued, "Hope Dad won't get into trouble for killing her, she started shooting first".

"You don't have to worry about your old man, replied Harris, "but you must understand that we will have to swear you to secrecy about some of the things you have seen and heard. It would be a treasonable offence for you to repeat anything we don't want you to".

Donald was a smart man, and voiced his understanding and assent.

Sergeant Biggs meanwhile realised that he had probably dropped himself in it with his comments to the boy, and had given the London man the moral highground again. Harris realised that Biggs realized this, so said nothing!!

Arriving at the police station, Harris waited for his subordinate to arrive. When he did so half an hour later, he advised that Judy Wilson was fine, and that she had also been sworn to secrecy regarding her statement.

"Sorry we have to speak to the lad alone sergeant", said Harris to Biggs.

"That's quite alright Sir", replied the local man, and turning to the desk sergeant said, "I think I'm well out of this Jim".

Donald related with clarity how he burst in on the two women with the intention of bringing Granny Wilson the rabbit. "But why not leave in in the box outside as your father normally does?, asked Harris. "Don't worry, he continued, "poaching isn't an issue here".

Don replied that he had seen the smoke coming out of the chimney, and thought he would surprise the old lady.

"What you didn't realise Don, was that Granny Wilson was expecting your Dad to leave her dinner in the usual place. She left a note there warning him that an armed woman was in her house", related Cartwright.

Donald was suitably surprised at this and said worriedly, "So it was probably my fault that the woman was killed?"

"I wouldn't say that Don, replied Harris, "if your father had been able to give the warning earlier the outcome may have been worse. We may have had to storm the cottage. At least Granny wasn't hurt".

Just then the desk Sergeant. advised that a call had come through from Bath, so Tim Cartwright went to take it.

Bill Harris continued with his questioning of Donald, and asked what the foreign woman had said and done.

"Well, when we got in the car, I reversed into the hedge and then let the tyre down to make it look like a puncture. She went crazy and ordered me to sort it out".

"You wanted to waste time? Good thinking", said the agent.

Don continued, "I made out that her petrol tank was empty, and had to fill it with a can in the boot, then when I got back in the car she had sort of changed, and I could see that she'd pulled her skirt up to show me more of her legs".

"Trying to seduce you eh? What did she say at that time"?

"Well, thought Don, "she mentioned that perhaps I ought to go to London with her".

"Can you think of anything else she did or said that could be important to us", asked the MI5 man.

"There was one thing she asked me, he replied, after thinking hard "she asked me if I knew what some sort of codename meant".

Harris started, "Can you remember what it was?", he asked hopefully.

"I have been trying to memorise it yes, it was ST6552", he replied.

"Is that all? asked Harris, nothing more?"

The youngster thought and said "Yes, I remember now, she said she was looking for something that a friend had hidden, but that he only wanted her to find it".

"Nothing more than that? And *did* you know what this code meant Don?"

"No Sir, no idea at all. Oh, one other thing. When she asked me this first I didn't understand what she had said, so she apologized and said that she had spoken in Spanish".

"Mmmmm, ok Don, that will do for now, go home and rest and thanks for your help".

"And Dad?", asked the younger Breck.

Before he could answer however Tim opened the door and called Harris out.

"Sir, he said, "Forensics have called. They have carried out an inquest on the girl and found a bullet in her brain - from a type that you and I use. Seems that she could have been dead before Breck shot her".

Harris looked washed out, "Yes Tim, I thought as much", was his only reply.

He then told Don he could go home, and he advised him that his father would soon be released.

The two agents went back into the interview room and sat down while they waited for a welcome cup of coffee to be delivered. Tim could guess what his partner was going through, knowing that he had killed probably the only witness there was who could lead them to the missing document. The fact that the gamekeeper had supposedly killed her meant little now, and Harris was not one to try to pass the buck.

"I am like you Tim, he said, "we don't draw our guns often, but when we do, we don't miss. I knew I had killed her as soon as I got off my shot, she gave me quite a target when she leant out of the car window".

"You had no choice Sir, she was probably no dud with her derringer either".

Cartwright continued, "So where do we go from here? Looks pretty bleak".

"She told the boy she was going back to London, which was probably a feint, replied Tim's superior, "but do *you* know what ST6552 could mean? That's the question she put to the kid, said she was looking for something hidden for her".

Cartwright shook his head, but assured his boss that he would give priority to finding out.

"Yes get on it, its about the only lead with have at the moment".

"Do you think she had given up the ghost and really did intend driving back to London Sir?", asked Cartwright.

Harris thought about this and eventually replied, "Well, we need to know what she needed the most, this document to take back to her controllers whoever they may be, to have it for herself to make money out of and perhaps get to Buenos Aries, or her freedom. You are probably right, but how and where did she get this codeword from?"

The next few days for both men were spent in following up the small leads they had, and Harris went to visit the Abbott of Downbury again, hoping that a full scale search of the school, monastery and grounds could be made. Harris knew he was unable to order this, and was on precarious ground, but the Abbott refused anyway saying, "I can assure you Mr Harris that in my opinion the document you are searching for has never been inside Downbury at all, but if someone has hidden it somewhere securely, which I doubt, then would that be such a bad thing?"

Harris knew he had a point there, and left it at that. He would subsequently make sure that any future Spanish connections with Downbury were monitored however.

Harris decided he must set up a investigation scene headquarters, so commandeered a couple of rooms at the local police station. A couple of weeks intensive investigations must be applied now to try to solve the mystery of where the document went, and how. Failure to do this would not go down well in London, and the case would have to be shelved indefinetly, with the dangers to the Government that this would imply.

One of the first things Harris did was to order a watch to be put on the AA man Eric Reed. A local CID man had been given this job, and he called the MI5 man with an update.

"He hasn't been approached as you ordered Sir, reported Sgt Blackmore, "but his activities do seem a bit strange. He certainly likes hanging around that Norton Hollow area for some reason".

"Good work Sergeant, replied Bill, "I will meet you there. Wait for me near the chapel and we can talk".

Blackmore pulled his unmarked Wolsley onto the space next to the chapel, and Harris was dropped off to join him minutes later.

"What do we have Blackmore?", he asked.

"I've been watching him for a couple of days now and also asked discreetly in the pub, said the detective. "He is seen quite a lot riding around on his combination, but hardly ever to report to his phonebox over there on the main road. See that slip road opposite Sir? He often rides down there from the top end, and doesn't come out again sometimes for an hour or more".

"I don't understand what you mean, there's no house down there is there?"

"No Sir, only a type of old farm building. They call it locally The Dolls House. It's been renovated somewhat and looks a bit like one from outside".

"Have you looked inside?", asked Harris

Blackmore replied in the negative, and they both moved off to walk up the lane from the bottom end.

Harris was surprised to see that the building was of two stories, and that the ground floor was more like a garage with large doors fitted to the front and rear.

"I can't see where else he could get to unless he rides his bike into here", commented Blackmore.

There was only a small padlock on the doors of the front end, and a key was produced that easily opened it.

Inside was a smell of petrol, and tyre marks on the concrete floor which were clearly from a motorbike and sidecar combination. Apart from a few empty boxes and cans the floor was empty, and Harris looked up to see the upper barn. A wooden staircase had been constructed, and the two detectives climbed up it. It was immediately evident that someone had been here recently, and probably slept too as a campbed was made up.

"Look here Sir, said the sergeant, "we could have a pervert on our hands".

Blackmore had opened two drawers of a kind of sideboard against one wall, and inside had found several photographs of nude and partly nude young women.

"Do any of them look under age Sergeant?" replied Harris.

The CID man crinkled up his nose as though he weren't enjoying his task, and after scrutinising the pictures said,

"I wouldn't say so Sir, but I would say that he took them himself".

"Who did Sergeant?", retorted Harris.

"This AA man I would think Sir. I can check with all the local chemists to see if he uses them for his developing".

"Unless", replied the senior man, looking around. "What's behind that door there?" he added, pointing to the rear of the building.

"Hmm, muttered the other, "this storey does seem shorter than the downstairs one".

The door was firmly locked however, and Blackmore asked if they should get a search warrant.

"Yes we should, replied the MI5 man, "but I won't tell if you won't!"

Their combined shoulders and feet soon burst the door open, and sure enough a dark room had been set up in there, complete with a red light bulb and all the equipment necessary to develop photographs.

Several prints were pegged out on a washing line to dry off, and Harris saw that some of them were of a pretty, dark haired woman, but it looked as though she had been snapped while sleeping.

Blackmore in the meantime had found more drawers to delve into, and in the dim red light could see several articles of female underwear.

"Looks as though our man has a regular little love nest here sergeant, declared Harris, "Or maybe something worse. I want this place watched continuously until the patrolman arrives. I want to catch him in here".

The Operations Room had another message waiting for Bill Harris when he got back there, and it was from Forensics.

"Mr Harris? Dr Haldane here from Forensics. Thought you might like to know that the young woman has had children, or at least a child".

"Thank you Doctor. No evidence of an abortion, or possibly a miscarriage?.

"In my opinion, no, none at all".

Harris expressed his thanks again to the medical man, and decided that his investigations must now take him back to London for a while, and that at least one person there must be interviewed by him.

Tim Cartwright was again left in charge of the local investigations, and at once got on to Bath Police to check if Eric Reed was on file anywhere, and to also to be given information of any local sex-related crimes that Reed could be associated with. Subsequently these enquiries drew a blank, which was a relief to the MI5 man, rather than a setback.

Bill Harris, once in London again called on his direct chief Ian Green, who had fixed up an interview for the two of them with the Duke of Avila. "What do you think of the Duke's involvement in all this Sir", asked Harris.

Green lifted his eyebrows and asked "Meaning?"

Harris continued cautiously, "Well, what if he was part of a plot by Franco to have this document stolen so that he could use it at a later date?"

"And all the murders and double crossings have been deliberately staged?", the chief asked.

"It's a theory that must be examined surely Sir", replied the detective.

"I am sure this was seriously considered by the PM and others, but I think it doubtful. Spain needs the West to accept Franco's regime more than ever at the moment, and the feeling is that General Franco is a proud man who wouldn't stoop to those kind of tricks. No Bill, my feeling is that the Spanish Left have been planning this move for some time, and that our late Arancha was indeed a type of sleeper here".

"And the Duke was taken in by her?, asked Harris.

"I would say so, answered his superior, "but we will find out this afternoon".

At around midday, the sound of AA Patrolman Reed's motorbike and sidecar was heard approaching, and two local uniformed police officers waited hidden in the trees lining the lane. The padlock on the door of the Dolls House was left in place, but not snapped shut. Reed got off of his machine and walked to open the door, the surprise showing on his face when he saw that the lock had been tampered with. He gave a quick look around him, and then decided that he must look inside the building. After all, he could have forgotten to snap the lock shut.

Reed could see nothing out of place, and the ground floor at least was empty. Climbing the wooden steps, he saw everything was in order, and felt lucky that no one had got in. Police officers had put the forced door to the dark room back in place as best they could, and as Reed walked back to the door he met one of those officers.

"Good afternoon Sir, said the constable, "would you like to turn your machine off please, some gentlemen want to have a word with you".

A squad car drew up with Sergeant Blackmore and Detective Cartwright inside.

Getting out and entering the building, Cartwright introduced themselves as CID men, and asked the AA man what he was doing in the building.

Reed was looking shaky, but quickly said, "I was riding past on my way to the patrol phone box, and just happened to see that this lock was open. Doing *your* sort of job", he added, laughing nervously.

"I don't think many of us share your job Mr Reed, or should I say your *hobbies*. Now Sir, because of your occupation we want to be discreet, so I want you to think carefully before I ask you another question".

Reed made to speak, but Cartwright signalled for him to stay quiet.

"Bear in mind Mr Reed that we have made a full investigation of this building, and have found a hidden darkroom, have lifted many fingerprints that seem to be from just one or two persons, and have eye witnesses who can testify who they saw entering this building. Now, the question is have you ever been in this building before?"

Reed look crestfallen and broken, but replied, "Yes, yes of course I have officer, but I haven't committed any crimes, and I have had permission to use this place".

Cartwright nodded to the uniformed officers and said, "Thank you Sir, now we would like you to follow us to the station, where we would like to ask you some more questions. If you have to ring in to your headquarters at all, you can do it from there".

The two constables went to where their patrol car was parked farther down the lane, and followed Reed and their superiors to the police station.

CHAPTER 15

After lunch MI5 men Ian Green and William Harris were shown into the private office of the representative of the Government of Spain the Duke of Avila.

The Duke welcomed the two agents warmly, and said, "What news do you have for me gentlemen? Has Arancha been found?"

"Well we aren't sure yet Sir, but we are hoping that you can throw more light on the matter so that we can finalise our search".

The Duke look suitably puzzled, but replied, "Of course, anything that can help".

Harris was the man on the ground, so took over the interview.

"Can you tell me Sir, in total confidence of course, what your relationship was with this woman, how long you have known her, and what exactly do you know about her". Before allowing the other to speak, Harris added, "I don't need to advise you Sir of the serious magnitude of this matter, so we have to have your frankest and most truthful answers".

Avila nodded his assent and started, "I am sure you know quite a lot already Mr Harris, and have the facilities to find out more. Very well, Arancha was an occasional friend, an intimate friend you know, but not my mistress. I have known her for several years, four or five I think. She was introduced to me at a party one day, but I don't know too much about her past, in Spain that is. I rather think she came to England to make a new start, perhaps to forget a lover?"

"She was definitely single?", asked Harris.

"Oh yes", answered the Spaniard a little too quickly.

Harris then dropped his bombshell. "Did you know that she had a child Sir?"

The envoy gripped the edge of his desk and looked shaken. After a long pause he looked the two agents in the eye.

"Yes, she had a daughter two years ago, but I wasn't the father, I swear that to you".

"And where is the girl now Sir?", asked Green, who edged in to the conversation.

Another painful pause came from the Duke before replying, "She is in Spain, I arranged for her to be adopted by a good family there".

"And you naturally assisted this family financially?", asked Green.

The Duke nodded. "And still do?" added Green.

"Yes, damn you yes". The Duke had finally lost his composure, and his temper.

Harris felt he should keep the pressure on the man now and took over the interview once more, "And why would you do all this for Arancha Sir? Didn't she want to keep her baby, or maybe it was interfering with her work?"

"I told you, replied Avila, "she was a special friend".

"Is it not true Sir that she was a prostitute? Maybe a classy one, but a prostitute?" asked Harris.

The Duke turned red, and looked as though he were going to choke with rage, "*Vale, vale, es una puta si*", he stormed.

"Was, is the operative word now Sir", replied Harris tartly.

The Duke sat down to stop himself shaking. "Do you mean she is....?"

"I am afraid she's dead Sir, yes".

"Was she killed by that swine who tried to blackmail me?", he asked, looking genuinely shaken.

Inspector Green spoke again, "If what you have told us is true Sir, and we have no reason to think it isn't, then I am afraid that you have another shock coming to you".

The Spanish envoy suddenly looked older than his years, but folded his hands together and listened to what was coming.

"The young Spanish woman you knew as Arancha was killed by police officers in Somerset, avoiding arrest. She was in fact an associate of Juan Pardo, the man who came to see you. We still have a lot of enquiries to make, but we think that Arancha was placed in the UK by the Spanish Republic in exile, and she has been a sleeper here all these past years. Her friendship with you was probably planned, at least parts of it, so you see why it's important that we get to the truth as far as you are concerned", explained Green.

"It is fantastic, replied the Duke, "I can't believe it".

Harris then told Avila how Pardo had tricked him over the kidnapping in Arancha's flat, and how, when she heard that Pardo was dead in Somerset, the woman had gone there herself to try to find the Gibraltar document.

"But, continued Harris, "I am still puzzled as to why you helped the girl so much, over her unwanted baby?."

The Duke thought before replying, "I suppose I was infatuated with her, I was jealous, and knew she had other *clients* too, but I had this special relationship with her and wanted to help her. Do you understand that detective?"

"I think I do Sir", replied Harris thoughtfully.

"Well Sir, cut in Green, "unfortunately we will need a full statement signed by yourself, to include full details of where and when the little girl was sent, and who else was involved in the move".

The Duke still looked stunned, and could only nod his agreement. Was something else worrying him?

"What is it Sir?", asked Harris.

"I was wondering that if these… these pigs knew so much about me and what has occurred here, might they not have found out about the whereabouts of the child? Could her guardians be in any kind of danger from them?"

Harris and Green looked at each other, and Green spoke, "I don't see why Sir, what would they have to gain from it? I doubt if the girl would have wanted, or been allowed to contact the child again, and what you did was a personal matter that probably her superiors were glad of".

Green then told the Duke that two officers would come in and type out his statement, and then he and Harris excused themselves.

"Probably afraid someone will find out about his involvement with the child, and blackmail him", suggested Harris caustically.

"Well, replied his boss, "let him stew in it. We'll see what he tells us in his statement":

"Not everything, I doubt. Either he was the father of Arancha's child, or she led him to believe he was", remarked Harris.

"Whichever way, it cost him, replied Green, "maintenance *or* blackmail".

CHAPTER 16

"So, repeated Tim Cartwright to his suspect, "after you picked up this Spanish woman you brought her back to the Dolls House, and offered to let her stay there the night?"

"That's right, replied the sweating AA patrolman. She told me not to ask her too many questions, and that she would make it worthwhile".

"And did she?"

"No she didn't, when I returned in the morning she had left", said Eric Reed self righteously.

"How long did you stay with her, and what did you do and say?", persisted the lawman.

Reed was brought a cup of tea, and Cartwright offered him a cigarette, taking one for himself.

"She told me she was very tired and needed to sleep, but that I should come back again in the morning", he told his interviewer.

"But you took photographs of her, why?", asked Tim.

"Because she was a lovely looker, and I had a hunch that she was just using me. I just wanted to keep the photos for myself that's all, the same as the… other things I have collected. They have all been given to me willingly you know", explained Reed.

"The underwear you mean? And the photos of the other women you have had in here?"

"Yes, but as I said, it was all consensual", he stressed.

"And did she ask you any questions?", continued Tim.

"Yes, she asked a weird question, she asked me if I knew what ST6552 was".

Cartwright felt his pulse quicken, "And did you?", he asked hopefully.

"No, replied the other, but I found out and was going to tell her in the morning".

"You did!", cried the lawman surprised.

"It wasn't too difficult", he replied.

"Well, what is it?" asked the detective impatiently.

"It's the number allocated by the Somerset and Dorset Railway to Eastcompton station. You know, they all have a location number".

Eric Reed was dismissed for the time being and allowed to carry on with his work, and was finished and at home by midnight.

The night was cloudy with very little moon, but hardly any wind. Around 1.30am a figure dressed all in black left his car in the lane just down from the Dolls House, and started to walk towards it. It was a man, and he was carrying a large canful of petrol. Approaching the building he smashed the glass in the only window that the building had, took the cap off the petrol can, and heaved it straight through the window. Then, looking around just to make sure no one was about, he lit a couple of matches and threw them through the window to land on the spilled petrol. Waiting to hear the whoosh, he quickly departed and drove off in his car.

Next morning Cartwright had an early phone call from his boss Bill Harris, "Morning Tim, sorry you couldn't get me last night. Hear you have some news for me, I will be taking the Bath train in an hour".

"Yes Sir, replied the junior, "and I have even more news. I'm afraid that Dolls House building where that fellow Reed had his *hideout* was burnt to the ground last night".

"Dear me, Harris sputtered down the phone, "do the local police have any idea how it started?"

"None at all Sir, he replied smirking, "and I don't think they will be investigating too much either".

"Shame", said Harris.

"A tragedy!", followed Cartwright.

Before departing London, Harris and Ian Green read the statement that the Duke of Avila had dictated and signed, and Harris whistled, "Here is that name Downbury again, he says here that the Abbott was instrumental in arranging the adoption of the baby to the family in Extremadura".

"Is that significant?", asked Green.

"I suppose not, replied the MI5 detective, "it seems logical on the face of it, and the Abbott hardly lied as we didn't question him about it".

"But the Duke certainly seems shaken up by it all".

"I'm not surprised, replied Harris, "but I think he has a lot of worries. For one thing he will be worried that news of his affairs with Arancha will get back to Madrid, and then he could have in the back of his mind that his enemies will further try to blackmail him over them. He could even be worried for the safety of the adoptive parents".

"Yes, I'm sure you are right Bill, but we have our orders and tasks clearly laid out and that's all we can concentrate on at the moment", stated Ian Green.

CHAPTER 17

Easthampton Railway Station was a fairly small one, although it had two platforms and sidings going to the nearby colliery. Built in 1874, Easthampton was just two miles south of Midsomer Hollow. A little ways north of the station the railway line passed through the double bore Eastcompton Tunnel, and then through the 40 feet deep cutting that was the site of the discovery of Juan Pardo's body.

When Harris and Cartwright visited the station around noon, it was a clear, cold but sunny day. A porter showed them to the Station Master's office, and the studious-looking Mr Montague welcomed them.

Harris began, "We are here as part of the investigations into the body that was found on the line near Midsomer recently Sir".

"Ah yes gentlemen, you would be from Bath Police?"

"No Sir, replied Harris, "we are from MI5 in London. My name is Harris, and my colleague is Mr Cartwright. We must ask you and your staff to be discreet about our visit, but we have a couple of important questions to ask".

Montague looked suitably impressed, put down his pen and took his reading glasses off. "Ask away", he said.

"How many staff do you employ here Sir?", asked Harris.

"Well, apart from myself there are two porters who work opposite shifts, and the signalman".

Harris went on, "We want to know if any foreign stranger has called to the station during the last two or three weeks".

"Possibly the man they found dead?", asked the Station Master.

"Possibly", answered Harris cryptically.

"Well, I never saw anyone myself, but I can remember Franks telling me about a stranger", replied Montague.

"And Franks is?", asked Cartwright, speaking for the first time.

"One of our porters, sorry. In fact, he is the one that you've just seen".

"Good, replied Harris, "can you ask him to come in?".

"Yes, it's quiet for a half an hour or so, I'll call him".

Dennis Franks confirmed that a foreign man had spoken to him about 10 days ago, and when shown a photo of the dead Pardo, he thought that it was the same person.

"So what did he say or ask you?", prised Harris.

"Well, he asked if we could collect and deliver messages or packages here, and I told him we could. He asked me where the line went in both directions, and he asked me about the tunnel, you know, the one going towards Mid Hollow".

"Did he seem particularly interested in the tunnel?", asked Harris.

"He did a bit yes Sir. Oh, and he asked about the train times, so I showed him the timetables", replied the porter.

"And did this man give you anything to keep, or did he leave anything here?", asked the detective.

"No Sir, like what?"

"A package, or documents or papers for instance?", replied Harris

Franks shook his head and said "No Sir, nothing at all".

Harris asked the stationmaster if there were any chance that the man could have got inside anywhere and hid an article.

"Not at all Sir, replied Montague, "as far as I know he never even went into the toilets, did he Franks?"

"He didn't Sir", was the porter's firm reply.

Harris looked at his partner thoughtfully then said to Montague, "Have you ever been inside the tunnel Mr Stationmaster?"

Montague replied in the negative.

"Who has, do you think?", Harris continued.

"Well", though Montague, "the railways maintainence foreman has of course, and some of his men".

"Can you get him on the phone for me?", asked Harris.

Tim Cartwright looked at his boss and said, "Does this mean what I think it does Sir?"

"Yes Tim, he smirked, "hope you aren't claustrophobic!"

Jim Steele was the chief Maintainence Foreman Engineer for the Somerset and Dorset Railway, and within a quarter of an hour of Montague's request, he had called Eastcompton Station and was talking to Bill Harris.

"But do you know how difficult it would be to hide something in a tunnel Mr Harris?", he asked. "The walls are smooth and unbroken, we make sure there are no cracks or holes etc".

"Hmmm, muttered Harris, all the same I would like to have a look inside".

"Well that could be arranged with Head Office if you make a formal request, but there are matters to be considered", replied Steele.

"Go ahead", prompted Harris.

"Well for a start, we would have to plan the inspection for when there are no services running of course".

"Of course, replied the detective, "you will know the timetables".

"The Pines Express runs through here at 10.30 and then again at 17.30, so we can put traffic blocks up between those times", he offered helpfully.

"I understand there are two tunnel bores Jim?" he asked in a friendily voice.

"That was the other matter I was going to mention Mr Harris, he replied. "I would think you would be interested in the up?"

"The up?", Harris repeated.

"Northward, going towards Midsomer Hollow and on to Bath. That would be the left hand bore looking towards that direction", Steele confirmed.

"How long is the tunnel?" asked Cartwright.

"Just under 70 yards, and the line starts to decline northwards", answered the engineer.

"Really?", asked Tim.

"Oh yes, from Rainston southwards there is a steep climb right up into The Mendip Hills. Down trains usually have double-headers, you know, two locomotives to give extra power", explained Steele.

It was agreed that a team comprising Steele and two of his men, with Harris and Cartwright would share an initial investigation of the interior of the tunnel . They arrived at the south portal of the tunnel just after The Pines had passed through on its way to Manchester. Cartwright was the first to walk through, and he was positioned outside the other end at the northern portal. The other four men, equipped with helmets and powerful torches commenced their search of the walls and ceiling.

As Steele had said, the walls were lined with smooth faced bricks that had no gaps or irregularities at all, and the ceiling was blackened by 70 years of steam and smoke.

One of Steele's men was the first to see it, a kind of canvas pouch that had been attached to the wall, obviously with a very strong adhesive. It looked like the kind of pouch that another, more official one might be held inside, and was of quite rough appearance.It had been attached to the wall, about two metres from the ground

Detective Harris rushed over to look, and was immediately disappointed to see that the pouch had been opened, and was empty!

"Shit!, he cursed, "we must be too late. What bastard has taken it?".

Suddenly a shadow appeared across the portal of the tunnel, and a rushing noise filled the air.

"Look out!", shouted one of Steele's men, and all four instinctly pushed themselves back against the walls as something was entering the tunnel at speed.

Harris's trained eye quickly saw that it was a rail push trolley, with a man working it down the slope. Before he had time to shout he heard a clunk on the rails, and the trolley was past him in a flash.

Turning his head to follow its path, he shouted out to Cartwright, but his voice was drowned by the sound of a pistol shot, and he was temporary blinded by a muzzle blast.

Tim Cartwright had heard the noises from within and stirred, so was well prepared when he also heard the pistol shot. Crouching down, he quickly saw the trolley come through the tunnel opening with a man standing up. The man looked at Cartwright in horror, seeing he had a gun in his hand. He swung his own round towards the lawman, but it was an uneven contest from a moving vehicle, and Cartwright put three bullets into the man's torso.

Falling down across the handle, man and trolley careered on down the line, but Cartwright ran into the tunnel to join the others.

"Who the hell was that?, he shouted, "I think I killed him".

"Good work Tim, replied his chief, "but I would rather have had him alive".

Before they could gather their thoughts and ask questions, they saw that Jim Steele had gone down.

The two workman were badly shaken, and by the torchlight looked very pale.

"I think Jim has been shot Sir", said one of them.

Harris bent down to look, and Steele said, "It's my leg, reckon I was lucky".

"I reckon we were all lucky Jim", he replied.

Harris instructed one of the workmen to quickly go to the signalbox and call for an ambulance.

"You Tim, walk on down the line and see if that trolley has stopped. If so, seal the scene until I can get more men there".

"Who was that bastard?, asked Cartwright, "And how did he know we were here?".

"That's what I intend to find out, replied Harris, "but I heard something fall on the lines. Look".

A largish stone had been dropped from the trolley by the intruder, and Harris could see that it had a letter tied around it. He picked the stone up and unwrapped the message, which he immediately saw was in Spanish.

"*Idiots, el documento no esta aqui, tengo yo. Y Marjorie también!*", *Llama este numero a las 20.00 horas 27743"*, it read.

"Tim, come back here quick!", Harris shouted at his partner. "We can send someone else after the trolley, look at this".

The junior detective saw the note which he couldn't read, but like his superior soon saw the Methodist Minister's name written there. He turned pale, and asked how they could get the note fully translated. "Get to a phone and call Downbury, someone there will help if we spell out the letters", suggested Harris.

"I'll do it Sir, my God, if she is in danger...."

While Harris arranged for local police to quickly find the runaway trolley and create a crime scene there, Cartwright's worst fears were realised. Someone had called the school from the signal box. The text of the message was quite simple in that it read, "The document is not here, I have it, idiots. And Marjorie too". Ring 27743 at 9 this evening".

"There must have been three of them all along Sir, said Cartwright, "this last one watching us, and trying a last ditch effort to extract money for the document... by holding Marjorie to ransom".

"That's what it certainly looks like Tim, replied his superior, "but that doesn't explain how he knows so much about how our investigations have developed".

Their conversation was interrupted by Sergeant Biggs who arrived with two constables, and promptly sent them down the line to take care of the trolley and its occupant. "Excuse me Sir, but it's just been reported to us that there was dynamite stolen last night from the local colliery explosives store", he said.

"And this is significant sergeant?", replied Harris shortly.

"Well, the runaway trolley also came from the colliery sidings. Whoever stole it was taking advantage of the temporary traffic block on the line" , said the sergeant.

Detective Harris looked round sharply and said. "Oh it's you Sergeant Biggs, yes that's interesting". Then he added, "Thank you Biggs, good work".

A radio car had been summoned for the two MI5 men, and was now waiting for them in Tunnel Lane, so the two detectives only had to walk up the bank to reach it.

"We'll drive past the chapel first Tim, just to see if Miss Knight is there and satisfy ourselves that this isn't just a hoax, said Harris, "do you know where she lives?.

"Marjorie?", asked Tim. "No afraid I don't Sir".

Just as they were leaving, one of the constables came running back up the line. "The trolley turned over only about 200 yards down the line Sir, he stated breathlessly, "must have been picking up too much speed and was over heavy on one side".

"And the man?", asked Bill Harris.

"Lying dead Sir nearby, looks like gunshot wounds in the chest", he replied, glancing at Cartwright.

"Did you see his face constable? Did he look foreign to you?, asked the MI5 man.

"I had a quick look at him Sir, replied the constable, but I wouldn't have said he was anything but Northern European. Light hair and eyes".

Harris thanked the police officer, and instructed Sergeant Biggs to arrange for the body to be taken to the police mortuary. "And no one is to touch it until I get there, except the forensics guys", he ordered.

"Strange, mused Cartwright, "two men found dead on the railway lines within a few hundred yards of each other".

"And neither of them killed at the spot they were found in Tim. I have a nasty feeling about this. Let's go".

CHAPTER 18

The police car stopped outside of the Hollow Down Methodist Chapel, and Tim Cartwright could see that the door was closed, so jumped out to make sure it was locked.

"You have a look around Tim, and perhaps ask in the pub if they have seen anything happening", instructed Harris.

"Where are you going Sir?", asked Tim.

"I'm going to see Mrs Dimmock, she was friendly with Marjorie Knight and may know where she lives. I won't be long".

Harris instructed the police driver to turn left off of the lane and drive up the track leading to Hollow Hall Cottages, the scene of Juan Pardo's fatal attack. Reaching the four back to back terraced cottages Bill Harris whistled, "Well, who do we have here?"

He had just seen Eric Reed's bright yellow Automobile Association motorbike combination parked outside. "Stay by the gate here son, he said to the driver, "and if anyone comes out ask them their names, and if they have seen the Methodist Minister lately".

Harris knocked on the door, and Alice Dimmock opened it. "Hello Mrs Dimmock, my name is Harris and I am Tim Cartwright's colleague". The woman looked vacant so he added, "He was the detective who came to speak to you and your husband, I'm very sorry to hear he died".

"Oh yes, yes, she uttered, thank you. He's not suffering now. Will you come in?"

"Thank you Mrs Dimmock, this won't take long, he said, "do you have company?"

He didn't need an answer as a rather abashed looking Reed came out from the living room.

"Go and sit down both of you, said the recently widowed woman, " I was just making Eric a cup of tea. You'll have one Mr Harris?

"Thank you, yes", he replied cheerfully. Looking at the AA man he whispered, "You didn't take long to get your legs under the table, did you Mr Reed?"

Reed coloured, and stuttered something about them being old friends and all that. "How old?", thought Harris, but said nothing.

When Alice came back, Harris asked them both when they had last seen Marjorie Knight, and if either of them knew where she resided.

Reed stated that he had heard of the woman, but that as far as he knew had never met her.
Alice Dimmock told the agent that Marjorie had visited her on one occasion since Ken's death, and that was probably about three days earlier.

"I believe she be from London originally, but I think she be renting a couple of rooms behind The Post. You know, the pub", she added to the confused looking official.

Harris turned to Reed again and asked if he had seen any strangers around at all over the last few days.

"Well yes, there was one man who approached me near our call box. He asked me the same question that you and the girl did".

"That being?", inquired Harris.

"About that damn railway again, why is everyone so interested in it?", he asked.

"What did he look like Eric?, asked Harris, "was he foreign do you think?"

"No, I wouldn't have said so", replied the AA man.

"And what did he actually say to you. What kind of accent did he have"?, insisted the detective.

Reed scratched his chin and remarked, "He sounded like a Londoner to me, but not a cockney as such, if you know what I mean. A bit like the way you talk yourself. He just asked me where the railway line ran, and how to get to Eastcompton".

"But he didn't ask you what that code number meant, the one the girl asked about?"

"No Mr Harris, he didn't ask that".

Bill Harris was feeling depressed and weary now with this case, and its outcome seemed as far off as ever.

"Let's find Cartwright", he said to his driver.

Tim Cartwright had also found out that Marjorie lived in rented premises at The Post Cottages, and learned from neighbours that she hadn't been seen since yesterday.

Harris joined him, and filled him in on his news.

"Then if this third person didn't ask about the code number, it's probably because he already knew what it meant, and knew that the document was in the tunnel. But how?", asked the junior detective.

"Someone must have told him, but no one knows apart from us two, said Harris. "But yes, there is someone else....", his voice trailed off.

"And if the man I shot wasn't Spanish, why did he write the note in Spanish?, queried Cartwright.

"I was thinking of that Tim, he replied, "I don't know much Spanish but wouldn't they write idiotas, and not idiots?"

"Quite right Sir, replied Cartwright, adding "I think!"

"And another thing, the continentals cross the stem of their sevens, but on the note they were written our way – 7".

"So, remarked Cartwright, our man tried to make us think he was an accomplice of Pardo and Arancha, but maybe he wasn't?"

"Indeed, replied his boss, "but now we are no nearer to finding the document, and we have a missing person on our hands as well".

"And possibly a fourth person involved Sir", said Cartwright, as more of a statement than a question.

"We have to find the minister first Tim, let's go back up to the chapel". He then stopped in his tracks, and suddenly looked worried. "What is it Sir?", asked Tim.

"I've just had a horrible thought Tim, but my dates may be out anyway. That building that was burnt down...."

"Oh no Sir, don't worry, she wouldn't have been taken there, the sergeant assured me that no one was inside when the fire was started".

Harris smirked and said, "And how was he so sure Tim?".

Cartwright looked suitably sheepish, and remarked that he didn't like to ask!

"That has put my mind to rest anyway, he replied, "let's go".

The windows of the chapel were quite high, and you had to peer through them on tiptoes, or get something to stand on. As well as that, the windows had patterned glass in them which made looking through them very difficult.

Cartwright found a large, round stone to stand on however, and nearly fell off backwards after taking a look inside. "Look Sir, through this corner pane, that looks like someone sat in a chair in there!"

"Harris peered through and said, "You're right Tim, bang on the window as hard as you can".

It was Marjorie, and as she heard the banging she turned to the window shaking her head. Bill

Harris could see that she had a gag tied around her mouth, but it didn't look as though her hands or feet were tied.

She had the attention of the two detectives, and looked to be earnestly warning them about trying to get in.

"It's Marjorie alright Tim, he said, "but she's been gagged and it looks as though her feet are tied to a length of something".

Cartwright made a quick move to the front door of the chapel, but a cry of "Don't, stay there", from his superior stopped him in his tracks.

"She's trying to warn us Tim", he said.

"That stolen dynamite, do you think?", asked Cartwright.

"Yes, that bastard has probably fixed up some type of timebomb on the door". As Harris said this, he felt the adrenaline flowing through him, and he had shaken off his weariness and depression. It was action he needed, even though a poor soul was in risk of her life. He must think now, and quickly.

They could see Marjorie shuffling along and pointing to the door, and anxiously shaking her head again.

"Her feet obviously are tied to something, but not long enough to let her get near the door or windows, said Harris. "Tim, he continued, "tell the driver to call his station and also the colliery. I want someone here who is used to being around explosives".

Cartwright stared at his boss. "To assist me", he explained..

When Cartwright returned, the two men started to discuss in detail this latest development.

"So, said Tim, "It looks as though our friend has put a bomb on the door which he intends to explode at 9pm, unless we pay him the amount he wants for the missing document he took from the tunnel. And we have to ring the number he gave us to find out what that amount is".

"In a nutshell Tim yes, that's it, but you can put that in the past tense as you shot our man dead", said Bill Harris.

"Under normal circumstances I would say I was glad I did Sir, but it leaves us with an even bigger problem now. Do we still call that number?"

"Yes we call it Tim, not quite yet, but well before 9pm and hopefully after we have Miss Knight safe".

"Do you think anyone will answer? Maybe he isn't working alone?".

"He isn't working alone Tim, replied his boss, "you can bet your life on that. Information has been leaked somehow, and as soon as we have Marjorie safe I will be doing some serious investigating".

"There are so many things we don't know at the moment Sir, for example, If there is another person involved, is he watching us now?"

"I doubt that very much, he will want to keep himself safe and ready".

"And how will he expect this thing to work, will he demand to meet someone with the money, and how will the chapel door be opened without setting off that bomb?"

"We will just have to see how things progress, hey what's that?"

Marjorie had thrown something against the window to attract their attention, and had a piece of paper and pencil in her hand. She had shuffled as near as possible to the two men, and Harris peered through the window and screwed his eyes to try to see what she had written.

"Round back is old entrance to cellar", she had written, and was pointing to the vestry/changing room, where presumably it came out.

Harris nodded his understanding, and the two men hurried round the rear of the chapel.

Underneath a load of rubbish, old furniture and the discarded harp, could clearly be seen some stone steps.

"Shall I call for some help Sir", asked Cartwright.

"No! Harris replied curtly. "this operation is confidential, don't forget that, and I don't want anyone else around here if there is a device primed".

It took them a couple of minutes to clear away most of the obstructions, and a further two to force the unlocked, but heavily jammed door to the cellar.

The cellar was short, about 12 feet long, and had obviously been used as a storage space. It smelled musty when the two MI5 men entered it, the ceiling was low and they had to duck their heads. Cartwright turned on the small torch he carried, and they could see some old benches and other odds and ends stored there. Neither man could see the exit though, but then Tim Cartwright's beam showed up what looked like a blocked up doorway.

"Hmm, if we can break this open does it open inwards or outwards?", he said, more to himself. Harris told his partner to shine the torch around the floor, and a flat, kind of metal fixing from a piece of furniture was spotted. It was hanging half off of a bench, and Harris had soon twisted it right off and started running it down the closed door joints. A gap was found, and a couple of jerks on the metal fixture wrenched the door open towards them. "Thank God, said Harris perspiring, "you had better stay here Tim".

"No way Sir, you go and do what you have to do, and I will see to the young lady"

"Not a bad choice Tim, replied Harris smiling, "I get to disarm the bomb, and you look after the lady in distress!"

"Well, replied his partner, "you were an expert at it during the war, and you *are* in charge here!!"

Bill Harris had in fact worked quite a bit with bomb disposal units, both in and out of the services, and a quick look at this device on the door showed him that it was quite amateurish, and easy to disarm.

The time clock was stopped, and the now harmless device was dismantled. "Very crude, he said, "made to give maximum fear to Miss Knight, but not even dangerous if the door was forced, only when the set time was reached".

Cartwright had taken the gag off the Marjorie, and was now struggling with the length of chain that had been fixed to her ankles.

Once free, the relieved Marjorie couldn't help but put her arms round Tim and kiss him. Cartwright blushed, and Harris smirked.

"There is a kettle in the vestry Mr Harris, I could do with a cup of tea", she said.

"I'll do it", volunteered Cartwright, and went off while his superior asked Marjorie exactly what had happened.

The man had come into the chapel just after Marjorie arrived at 10 am, and surprised her from behind. Gagging her first with his hand, she felt him sliding the cold chain around one of her ankles. He was wearing a neckerchief over the lower part of his face, but she would recognise his eyes again, she said.

"He spoke in a London accent, and told me not to struggle or else I and others would be hurt. He said he was going to gag me with a scarf, but that the chain would prevent me from getting to the door or windows. Then he showed me the bundle of dynamite that had a clock attached to it. He was fiddling with it by the door for about five minutes, then asked me for the door key and told me not to shout out". Marjorie took a sip of the tea that Cartwright had brought her, then continued, "He said that I would be alright provided he was given what he was asking for, and then left. I heard him lock the door after him".

Just then the police driver shouted out that Harris was wanted on the radio.

"It's alright constable it is safe now, but I will be right out", he shouted.

It was Ian Green, Harris' superior in London, "Bill, in view of these new developments I'm coming down to Somerset. Should be there this evening, will tell you more later".

"Yes Sir", replied a pensive Bill Harris.

Going back into the scene of the recent hostage attempt, Harris told his subordinate to take charge of things here, while he went to Bath station to call someone in London.

"Shall we fetch a woman PC for you Miss Knight?" he asked Marjorie.

Marjorie laughed and said, "No Mr Harris, I'm ok, honestly".

Harris looked at Cartwright and replied, "Well you are in good hands anyway!"

CHAPTER 19

Once in the police station he got a line for London, and asked for Hugh Lorimer who was a journalist and personal friend. He was also a mine of information, and what he didn't know he could soon find out.

"Hugh, Bill Harris here".

"Hello Bill, I hear you are down in the sticks, how are doing?"

"None of your business Hugh, he replied, "you wouldn't want to know".

"Well if it's interesting enough, I will find out eventually", he laughed back.

"Listen Hugh, will you do some digging for me? Maybe then one day, I can tell you something about muckspreading!"

"Sounds as though you want to do some of that anyway old friend, fire away", chuckled Lorimer.

"I would like you to find out if anyone prominent in the City is in dire straits. You know, in debt, possibly being blackmailed, that kind of thing. Perhaps you can check the casinos, or local bookies to see if anyone has been gambling heavy and losing".

"What sort of *prominent people* Bill?" asked Lorimer.

"I think his creditors would be only to happy to tell you that, but rather than politicians, I was thinking of Heads of Departments, if you get my drift", replied the MI5 detective.

"Give me two or three days Bill".

"I can only give you one day Hugh, replied the agent, "this really is important. Will you do your best and call me back this time tomorrow?"

"Ok Bill, but don't expect too much. Speak tomorrow", replied Lorimer, and rang off.

Harris sat down at the station desk allocated him, and decided to put down on paper all the recent developments, so that he could make some sense of them. It took him a full five minutes though before he could put pencil to paper:

Arancha hears of Juan Pardo's death in Somerset and comes down here to look for the document – Pardo must have called her and contacted her somehow, to give her a vague set of numbers – presumably as he hardly thought his life was in danger, but that his freedom could have been. Why didn´t he tell her more though, and tip her off that the document was hidden inside the railway tunnel? Security? Didn't really want her to know too much?

Arancha is armed and dangerous, but is killed in a shoot out with us. Reed spends time with Arancha a couple of days before she is killed, and she asks him about the code. Reed subsequently finds out what it means, so the agents and helpers search the tunnel and find the hiding place empty. An unknown man then rides through the tunnel disturbing the seekers, throws down a message, and fires a shot which injures the railway engineer. – Who is this mystery man who was shot dead by Cartwright after emerging from the tunnel? How did he know about the document's hiding place? What did he do with the document? Harris scratched his head and tried to fathom out all the other questions he needed to answer:

Was this man in league with Pardo and Arancha? Harris doubted it.

Was he the same man who stole the dynamite and push trolley from the nearby colliery? Almost certainly, he thought.

Who tipped off the mystery man about using the Methodist Minister as a hostage? Harris had an idea, fantastic as it seemed.

How was the hostage situation supposed to have worked? The timeclock on the homemade bomb was set for 11pm. and the telephone call for 9pm. Would mystery man have really exploded the bomb if he didn't get what he was asking for – presumably money in exchange for the document? Hard to say, thought the MI5 detective, but probably yes if there were yet someone else involved, someone with the brains.

If there is someone else involved, will he still try to extort money in exchange for the document, now that mystery man is dead? How did he find out that mystery man is dead? Does he know the current hiding place of the document, and if not, will he use bluff to get what he wants? "Impossible to answer at this stage", thought Harris aloud.

Tim Cartwright had seen Marjorie Knight home, telling her to stay there until the morning, and now joined his superior in the police station.

"Tim, said Harris, "I forgot to tell you to cancel that explosives expert".

"No worry Sir, I did it, he replied,, "told them it was a false alarm".

"Good lad, if my hunch is right we must make that phone call tonight at nine. If someone else is involved, it will be paramount that no one knows that Marjorie is free. You have your men stationed?

Cartwright nodded, "CID men and local bobbies are well concealed, and will work in shifts all night if necessary. They will know if anyone comes near to the chapel".

"Good", replied Bill Harris.

"When is Mr Green arriving Sir? Is he going to take command?, asked the junior agent.

"I have a feeling we may see him this evening Tim", was all that Harris would say.

"I know this may sound obvious Sir, said Cartwright mischieviously, "but can we not try to locate the phone number our man gave us on his message. And couldn't we try it now?"

"No, but it's good thinking though Tim. The local CID have told me it's almost impossible to trace the number. They can only do that with an incoming call, and then it isn't easy". Harris looked thoughtful, and then added, "As for ringing the number before 9pm. Well, there is no danger to the young lady now, but our man, if there is one, may be suspicious that we have rung early".

"But if he wants to make a deal and have his money...." replied Tim.

Harris thought again and uttered, "Let's do it".

First though he had an idea. Earlier that year EMI had brought out their new BTR1 tape recording machine, and MI5 Headquarters in London had one. "I will try to get our call connected to London and recorded Tim. Trouble is that Ian Green is not there, and I want it sorted out before he arrives here".

"Who else is there Sir, asked Cartwright, "Ian Burton? He's the technical wizard."

"Not another bloody Ian!" answered his boss caustically, "I think you're right though, I'll call him".

Half an hour later the wizard Burton thought that he had everything arranged. He was only too pleased to put his new *toy* into operation, and by the sound of it, to have Green off his back too. He was also a close friend of Tim Cartwright, which could prove useful.

"But Sir, said Burton to Bill Harris, "it can't be done I'm afraid, Inspector Green has left a message that the machine isn't to be used until his return. It looks as though he has a similar idea to yourself, and has it connected to a telephone line".

Bill Harris turned to Cartwright and said, "Maybe to playback later in the evening when Burton and everyone else has gone home".

Tim Cartwright was beginning to get his boss's drift.

"Listen Burton, he said to his man in London, "I'm going to ring a number, and you tell me if anything happens there".

Harris dialled 27743, the phone rang six times, then a crackly connection tone was heard and a voice said, "Listen carefully, at 11pm tonight a bomb will be exploded in the building where we have our hostage held. To avoid this happening, and to get the document you desire, you will pay me 5.000 pounds. When you have the money ready, in used banknotes, call this number again and I will give you instructions".

An excited Burton shouted down the phone, "A recorded message. What does it mean Sir?"

"A recorded message!" shouted Harris and Cartwright in unison.

Then to Ian Burton again he said, "Not a word of this to anyone Burton, not even to Inspector Green. Is that clear?"

"Well yes Sir, of course", he replied, rather surprised.

Just then the door was opened a shade, and the desk sergeant put his head through. "A call for Detective Harris from London, on this line here Sir".

Hugh Lorimer's cheery voice came on the line, "Hello Bill old pal, Hugh here, are you ready for a surprise?"

"Hit me", replied the MI5 agent.

"One Ian Green, his is the name that keeps coming up. He's high up in some government department or other, and apparently is a big gambler, a poor one at that".

"Good work Hugh, what have you found out?, pressed Harris.

"He owes quite a few hundred pounds to two largish casinos at least, maybe more. And oh, he seems to be on the point of starting a lengthy, and costly divorce from his wife".

"Thanks again Hugh, I'm grateful, said Harris, "but this is deadly secret, and I will have your balls if you share this with anyone else".

Lorimer laughed, but he knew when to keep quiet.

"What I can't understand, said Cartwright to his boss after being told the information, "is how the blackmailer expects anyone to get 5.000 pounds between the hours of 9pm and 11pm?"

"I know Tim, it all sounds ludicrous to me, but we will have to see what unfolds this evening. We'll have a bite to eat now, and I want to think about our next move".

"Do you really think Inspector Green has anything to do with the hostage situation Sir?", asked Cartwright.

"I'm afraid it looks that way Tim, but he should be arriving soon, so it will be interesting to see if he contacts us straight away".

"What will you tell him?, asked Tim, "the truth that Marjorie has been freed, or keep quiet and call his bluff?"

"Let's get that food Tim. We both need a beer to help us think!", replied Harris.

CHAPTER 20

The two detectives lit up their smokes after a good meal, and ordered a brandy each.

"Let's suppose Ian Green did set up this situation Tim, uttered Harris, "Did you check with Ian Burton if there were any other taped messages ready to be heard?".

"Yes I did, replied his partner, "there was only the one message, and Burton has the tape recorder under lock and key so no one else will have access to it".

"That's good, replied Bill, "but it does mean that Green wasn't expecting anyone to ring back again after 9pm. There is obviously more to this than meets the eye".

Bill Harris put his glass down and had decided, "Tim, he said, "go out to the radio car and tell the driver to come in and have his lunch. Afterwards, call Bath station and ask if they have been instructed to send a car out to the the railway station to collect Ian Green from the Paddington train. I will be out shortly".

The driver constable came in, and was suitably pleased when Harris said, "Sit down and have some lunch driver, I recommend the pie and chips. On my account ok?"

"Thanks very much Sir", he replied.

"I'm going out to your car constable, we need to use the radio", added Harris.

As the MI5 man left the pub, he looked up at the darkening sky. "Looks like rain Tim, it's getting very dark".

"A storm forecast Sir, replied Cartwright, "I've phoned Bath, no car ordered for Inspector Green".

"Hmmm, thought Harris, give me the radio Tim".

"Hello this is Detective Harris, can you put me through to Inspector Markham of your CID?" Markham was in the station luckily, and Harris asked him, "Please listen carefully Inspector, you already know that the case we are on is delicate".

"Of course, answered Dave Markham, "go ahead". Markham was a dapper officer, always immaculately dressed in well fitting suits, and with his trade mark fancy ties!

"I want you to observe one Ian Green coming off the 13.30 Paddington train. Don't approach him or let him see he is being tailed, just report to me where he goes, and what he does. Ok?"

"Yes ok, but who is he Mr Harris?"

Markham was unsure whether he should call Harris Sir, or not, but he was left in no doubt when Harris replied.

"He's a detective in MI5 like me, and yes Inspector, we both outrank you", he laughed down the phone.

"Of course Sir, laughed Markham with him, "I will get my sergeant to assist me".

"Good man", replied Harris, and proceeded to give Markham a description of his superior.

Markham thought about wearing a raincoat to hide his clothes, but would be found to need it anyway.

Ian Green jumped out of the train as it came to rest on the Chippenham platform, and he had enough time for a quick coffee before continuing the last fourteen miles to Bath by motorcoach. It had been a worrying day for the MI5 Section Chief, and the worst of it was still to come. Bill Harris had told him that young Cartwright had shot dead the mystery man who attacked them in the railway tunnel, and presumably stolen the Gib document. That was good news for Green, as far as he should be able to collect the document where it had been re-hidden, and return to London with it without anyone knowing. He should then be able to put into action his second plan of asking for money in exchange for the precious document, with the authorities still none the wiser as to who was really behind the plot. The difficult part was going to be the meeting with Harris and Cartwright.

Meanwhile in Bath the shot man's identity had been discovered, and his past was being scrupulously investigated.

Harris and Cartwright entered the police station, and were glad to get out of the wind and rain, which was now falling heavily.

Sergeant Biggs again shook hands with the two detectives, and said, "He is Gerald Tanner Sir, was actually a sergeant in the Sappers during the war. A bit of a tough nut by all accounts, and has a police record".

Harris saw the paper in Bigg's hand and asked to see it.

"A suspended prison sentence for stealing and handling explosives, and a caution for wounding. Suspected of being an accomplice to a bank robbery, but no firm proof. Seems our man has a fairy godfather to look after him", uttered the agent. "Interesting".

"It has been proved that he was the one who broke into the colliery stores and took explosives, and also the push pull trolley".

"Yes Sergeant Biggs, thank you", replied Harris, not wanting to discuss things too much.

The officer on the desk suddenly said, "Call for you Mr Harris".

It was Inspector Markham, "Nothing to report Sir. Inspector Green wasn't on that train, or at least he didn't get off it at Bath".

"Clever", muttered Harris after putting down the receiver.

Green sat in the bus shelter, hearing the rain pound down heavier still on the corrugated roof. His mind went back to what first got him into this mess. It was easy to blame his wife for her unsympathetic attitude towards his work, his long hours away from home, and his abandonment of her. Gradually, over the last couple of post war years the couple had grown apart from each other until their relations had become decidedly icy. Then came the gambling and drinking, he trying to find solace or diversion. He had a good position and reputation, and it was easy to slip into the nightclub and casino life of the West End. Credit was afforded him without trouble, and the casino visits and the debts increased, until he had to find a way out before someone high up found out and his position as Section Chief of MI5 be compromised.

While cross checking files with another department a few months ago, Green came across one for Gerald Tanner, and it hinted at his possible involvement with a Russian contact while in Berlin in 1945. Green kept the information under wraps, but sought Tanner out and decided that he could be useful to him personally, rather than to the department.

A plan was hatched that he, Ian Green, would try what at least three people had been killed attempting to do, namely to get hold of the document compromising the UK government over Gibraltar, and extorting money for its return. He would have to be very careful though, as Bill Harris was a shrewd and clever detective. As nothing had been heard from Tanner, he must either have been apprehended or eliminated by the two MI5 agents Green had assigned to the job. The second possibility would be a perfect solution for Green, Tanner would be blamed for the hostage attempt without any link to himself. He would then be able to get the Gibraltar document from where Tanner agreed to leave it... in a left luggage box at Bath railway station. If however, Harris and Cartwright should arrest and interrogate Tanner, there was a slim chance that he would break down and talk, but that was unlikely in view of the carrot and stick that he had been shown.

The worst part was not knowing what had happened recently since Harris's last update. Hopefully the girl hadn't been harmed and was now released, and his two agents were puzzling over the whole affair.

"Well then, he thought, "as soon as I get the document I can stand them down and tell them that we have come to a dead end in the investigation. If only this rain would ease off though".

The rain didn't ease off, far from it as a storm was beginning. The sky was now becoming dark all over, and the rain was being whipped into the faces of people who were not under cover. The wind was getting to be galeforce and dangerous, and Green could see that the streets were now practically deserted.

Over the bus station intercom travellers were being advised of delays for incoming and departing buses and coaches, and there was some mention of fallen trees on the road to Bath. Things weren't going well for the MI5 chief, departures to Bath were being confirmed as delayed or cancelled and he was anxious to get to Bath to retrieve the document. He could then go back to London without meeting his subordinates, on the premise that he had to abort his journey due to the bad weather.

A small group of passengers were chatting to a man and seemed to be quite animated. Ian Green approached them and overheard some of the conversation, which seemed to be revolving around the possibility of a van driver taking them on to Bath. He heard someone say that all train services had been disrupted, and there were long delays going both west and east.

"I need to get to Bath quite urgently", said Green to no one in particular.

"We all do Mister", replied a man with a large suitcase.

The person who they all seemed to be thronged around turned, and Green saw that he was a black man.

"Are you the driver of the vehicle I overheard these people talking about. Can you take me to Bath?"

The man was tall and heavy, and spoke with a American accent. "We are just discussing that Sir, he replied with a slight touch of irony, "but there were several people here before you".

"Of course, ceded Green, "but is it possible?"

"If it's worth my while I guess I can get through ok, but as I say, it would have to be worth my while", said the American cagily.

"I will pay you well, said Green, "but are you sure we have a chance of making it?"

The American faced Ian Green again and told him that that was impossible to say. "I can only try mister. I was here in 1944 preparing for the big push to France, and I was in charge of transport section, so I guess I know most of your country lanes here as well as anyone!"

The MI5 chief shook his hand and said, "Well I would like to take the chance with you Mr..?"

"Dodd, Crawford Dodd. And yours Sir?".

"Umm Nolan, Geoffrey Nolan", lied Green.

"When can we start then Mr Dodd?", he asked.

"Dodd took a good look at the other man and replied, "Seems like you are anxious to leave Mr Nolan, so I will take ten pounds from each of you who wants to come, and I can take four of you".

While the others were deciding, Green called Dodd aside, "Listen, there will be more money in this for you if you can do me a small favour when we get to Bath, and I may pay you to bring me back again".

"Back to here, to Chipping Ham?", was how the American pronounced the town's name.

"No, not here, possibly to London. Are you game?"

Dodd stretched himself to his full six feet three and gave a loud laugh, "Hell, lets get to Bath first mister, then we'll talk!"

CHAPTER 21

The vehicle in question was a brand new Bedford PC van, and when it was observed by most of the prospective passengers, the trip was politely turned down by them as probably to be *too uncomfortable*. One other man apart from Ian Green was keen to make the trip however, so Dodd told them he would accept twelve pounds apiece from them, with no guarantee of getting through. As the two men paid over their *fares*, the thunder and lightning was almost overhead.

"Let's get going", said the American, putting the men's luggage in the back of the van. "You can both sit in front alongside me, six eyes are better than four in this weather!"

As they pulled out of the bus station the roads were practically empty of traffic, except for one or two brave souls. Large pools of water were gathering on the insides of the roads, and trees were being bent into incredible angles by the wind.

Leaving the town centre they came across two fallen trees, but although the weather was yet too bad for workmen to be sent out to clear them, Dodd was able to negotiate his way through the roads which were reduced to one lane.

Things were too tense for small talk, and the big American put all his concentration into driving.

Green felt for the left luggage ticket that Tanner had mailed him, and turned over in his mind what his next moves were to be when reaching his destination.

The sky was actually clearing a little, and the wind abating as they saw the portal of Box Tunnel.

"Best place to be in a thunder storm, in a tunnel", exclaimed Dodd suddenly. It was the first time he had spoken since the journey began.

"Anyone like a cigarette?", asked Green.

"Why thank you Mr Nolan, replied Dodd, I think we are past the worst of the storm. I reckon we will be there in half an hour or so".

The other man who was called Jacobs also took a Players, and the three smoked in silence. Dodd turned his face round to get his smoke lighted, and the van suddenly hit a great puddle of water which careered onto the windscreen. Struggling to get control of the heavy van, the engine then cut out on him

"Must have got water on the electrics somewhere, he said to the others cursing his luck, "I'll have a look".

All three got out, but the weather was still bad so the driver told them to get back in while he lifted the bonnet.

"We'll wait 10 minutes or so and then try to start her up", he shouted against the wind.

Jacobs had finished smoking his cigarette and was dozing off, while Ian Green was getting more and more anxious.

"Ok gents, let's try her now", said Dodd sliding into the drivers seat. The van started first time, much to their relief.

It was dark when they pulled into the Bath Spa railway station carpark, and Jacobs alighted after giving his thanks.

Crawford turned to his other passenger and asked, "Well Mr Nolan, you said you had another job for me?"

"Look Dodd, explained the other, "first of all would you please take this left luggage ticket and bring me what you find inside the box?"

The American started to speak, but Green put his hand up. " Please, if you will do this for me I will explain and make things worth your while". With that he gave the ticket to Dodd, who didn't look quite as puzzled as he should have been.

Turning up the collar of his overcoat, the big American faced the wind and rain which was still fierce, and found the left luggage office. In exchange for the key he opened the box, and saw inside a single sheet of paper folded over, but not in an envelope. Quickly running his eyes over it he read, "Need more guarantees from you, I've taken the risks. Document safe and shock-free".

A smile came over Dodd's face as he slowly walked back to the van.

Green saw the piece of paper and said worriedly, "Is that all there was? Wasn't there any other documents or an envelope?"

"No Sir, replied the driver, "that was all there was in the box".

The M15 chief read the note and his face fell. "That filthy double-crosser..."

"Sir?", asked the other.

"No, no nothing he replied, just let me think a little"

"Of course Sir, I'm going to get me a cup of your rotten British coffee", he drawled, can I get you something?"

There was no reply forthcoming, so Dodd left the van again.

"No, no thank you", Green called after him.

"Shit, thought Green, "what the hell do I do now? He could have left that damned document anywhere, and I'm back to square one".

Crawford Dodd came back a few minutes later with a steaming cup of tea and a rock cake. "Thought you could do with this anyway Sir", he said, handing the refreshments over.

The worried looking Green sipped his tea in silence. Dodd waited, then said, "Did you say you wanted me to drive you back again Sir? I think the weather may be improving".

The London man looked crestfallen and nodded. "Yes please, I have to, I must get back to London. Will you take me?"

"Of course I will Mr Green, it will be my pleasure", Dodd replied, looking at the other to see his reaction.

That was slow coming, but suddenly Green looked the other in the face and asked, "What did you call me? My name is Nolan".

"I don't think so Sir, I think your name is Ian Green, and I've been on your trail for a while now. Shall we leave, or would you like your colleagues to come and collect you?"

"But I don't understand, who are you?", he almost cried.

"My name is Crawford Dodd, like I told you Mr Green, but I am attached to US Intelligence. You could say we are well, almost cousins!"

Green relaxed. "The OSS?", he asked.

"No Sir, we were the Office of Strategic Services, but since last year we became the Central Intelligence Agency. I am one of their agents in your country Sir. The world is a dangerous place at the moment".

Green was confused. "But you mentioned my *colleagues* just now, what did you mean? And you said that you have been on my trail?"

Dodd rubbed his great hand on his chin and spoke. "I will come clean with you Mr Green, I know that your two underlings are down here in Somerset investigating a few murders and a missing document, and I'm here investigating you!"

Ian Green felt a sinking feeling again, "What does our investigations here have to do with your country, and how dare you say you are investigating me?"

"Braze it out all you want Mr Green, replied Dodd, "I have called the police, and they no doubt will be contacting your collegues. You must have been very disappointed not to find what you had hoped to in that left luggage box – and your Russian masters will be even more disappointed I guess!"

The disgraced MI5 boss could see the writing on the wall, so slipped the automatic pistol from his inside jacket pocket. "Out", he ordered the big CIA man.

"Fine, replied Dodd casually, "you won't get very far what with the weather, and the police on your trail".

Green repeated his order and brandished his pistol in the other's face, "I said get out of the van, slowly".

Dodd chuckled, "Don't you think I am armed too Mr Green? I could have got the drop on you a few minutes ago... what do you call it, a *citizen's arrest?*" Wouldn't have looked good for a foreigner to be armed, though I thought you may have behaved more sensibly in the circumstances Mr Green".

"Get out, and stand well back from the vehicle", ordered the Englishman.

Crawford Dodd did as he was told, and the other started up the engine and pulled away jerkily. A police radio car pulled up a few minutes later, and after speaking to the American the driver flashed out a description of the stolen van. All of Bath's exit roads would be sealed within minutes.

"Did you contact the other investigating agents?", asked Dodd.

He was advised that Bath CID had contacted agents Harris and Cartwright, and that they were on their way.

"Please come with us to the station Sir, you can explain everything there".

"Not to you I won't", thought Dodd, then replied, "Will this Harris and Cartwright be there?"

"Our Inspector will answer all your questions Sir", was all the police sergeant would say, and told his driver to proceed.

Inspector Markham was no fool though, and he only asked the American a few general questions while waiting for the MI5 agents to join them.

This took nearly an hour though as the weather was still bad, and tea was brought in for Dodd and Markham just as the two arrived.

"Make that two more cups constable", said the Inspector as Harris entered the interview room.

"Thanks Inspector, we can do with it, said Harris, "Tim is briefing your desk sergeant, if that's not a problem?"

"No of course not Mr Harris. This is Mr Crawford Dodd from the United States, perhaps you need to talk with him on your own?"

They both understood each other, so Markham took the hint and said that he would go and take over from the desk sergeant.

Bill Harris extended his hand to the other, and Dodd stood up and shook it. He wasn't expecting a black man, and he wasn't expecting this one to be so big!

"My name is Bill Harris Mr Dodd, and I am a Senior Agent for our security services. I believe you have spoken to a Mr Ian Green, who you suspect of breaking the law in some way?"

"Crawford Dodd Sir, from the CIA. Do you know of it?"

"Yes I do, replied the other, "Criminal Investigation Agency. Perhaps we should show each other our credentials?"

Dodd chuckled and got his badge out, while Harris did the same.

"Sit down Mr Dodd, before our tea gets cold".

Dodd laughed again,"It's true what they say about you Limeys, everything can be solved over a damn cup of tea!"

"And you Yanks?", Harris laughed back.

The CIA man suddenly fell serious and said, "Mr Harris, I'm putting my cards on the table. We know Ian Green was Field Chief of your organisation, your MI5, but we have had him under surveillance for some time Sir, on suspicion of passing on information to the Russians. We don't know exactly what you guys have been investigating down here in the West of England, but we do know that there have been a few suspicious deaths and fire fights. We are also fairly sure that..."

"You have a damn cheek....", Harris cut off the American, but Dodd insisted in continuing.

"I was saying that your investigation is almost certainly connected to Mr Green's subversive activities. We know that he, and a man whom he had some sort of hold on, have been passing on classified information to the East for at least eighteen months now. We know this, because we have our own man infiltrating the Russians".

"And this man he has a hold on?",asked Harris.

"Tanner, Gerald Tanner. You know him of course?" answered the American.

"Know of him, yes. But you had Ian Green here, and let him go? How did he get to Bath, we were expecting his train".

"I brought him here Mr Harris, I have been snooping around between here and London, and got a good disguise as an unofficial taxi driver", laughed Dodd. "I'd spotted him at Chipping Ham before he saw me, and well, the rest just sort of happened better than I had expected".

"And he has stolen your van? Well he won't get far, that's for sure".

CHAPTER 22

Ian Green knew this too, the police would have roadblocks all around the city, and anyway there was very little traffic on the road at this time of night and in this weather. He didn't know Bath very well, but had studied a road map of the inner city before leaving London, and he also knew that Bath had a second, smaller railway station that served the Somerset and Dorset Line going South. The police would be expecting him to attempt to drive the stolen van out of the city, and probably back to London. Instead, Green stayed inside the city and attempted to find the other railway station, but by keeping to side streets as much as possible. He soon found signs showing directions and boldly made for his destination, then luckily through the murky weather saw what looked like a row of garages or lock-ups. Getting out of the van he felt the rain hit his face, and started to walk up the row of buildings. The third one up was locked by just a flimsy padlock on an equally flimsy hasp and staple. Green had noticed a few tools in the back of the van and went to fetch a screwdriver, with which he had soon prised the fastenings from the wooden door of the lock up. The inside was completely empty and quite clean, so after checking the street, he went to the van and drove it in. Then, he put the door fastenings back together again on the outside of the door, and hoped that no one would look at it too closely until the morning.

Back in the police station Tim Cartwright had been called into the interview room, and had been filled in on the latest news.

"It pisses me off a bit to think that you Americans suspected our own chief, and we knew nothing", he said.

"But you did suspect him Mr Cartwright, replied Dodd, "that's why you were trailing him yourself. And you would certainly have found out about his spying activities before long. As I said, we had inside information about that".

"I know what Tim is saying though, put in Bill Harris, "and you could have tipped us off before".

"Not possible I'm afraid, replied the CIA agent, we weren't entirely sure who to trust and who not to".

"As a country, or as individuals Mr Dodd?", asked Harris.

Crawford Dodd laughed his loud laugh again and said, "See here gentlemen, they say that you Brits taught our security services all they know, but unfortunately you didn't teach us *all that you know*!"

The two MI5 men appreciated this, and Harris asked Dodd if he thought the fugitive would try to drive back to London.

"Empty handed?", he replied, "I don't think so. I saw the note that was left for him at the station, and it could have given him some kind of clue as to the whereabouts of what he is seeking".

"Well, replied Harris, we will keep in touch over developments", and he and Cartwright took their leave of the American.

The two went outside to where a patrol car was waiting to take them to their accommodation.

"We have a lot of thinking to do Tim. If Ian is a spy, it's probably because of his financial troubles, and if he wanted the Gibraltar agreement so that he could sell it to the Russians, then that puts a completely different slant on things", said Harris.

"But who do we consult with now Boss?", asked Cartwright.

"Well, you consult with me Tim", Harris mumbled, "And as for me, 'lll have to see what develops!"

In the lock up garage Ian Green left the van's sidelights turned on, and retrieved some of the belongings from his holdall. A change of dress from his suit, a wig and a pair of thick black-framed glasses were extracted. Satisfied that his appearance had changed sufficiently, Green turned his mind to getting something to eat and drink. The railway station cafeteria was nearby, so he eased open the garage door, saw no one was around, and slipped out. He was now wearing a gabardine mack over a jacket and trousers, and his hair was now a shade darker and less wavy than before.

As he approached the cafe Green saw a constable patrolling the platform, but he wasn't challenged. Feeling relieved, he sat down in the cafe and ordered a hot meal, and also some sandwiches to take away with him. Before leaving the station he checked the times of the morning trains, then fifteen minutes later was safely back inside the garage where he settled down to sleep inside the van.

He slept fitfully for a few hours, but by six o'clock woke up stiff and feeling dirty. He ate his sandwiches, risked smoking a cigarette, then proceeded to clear up all his belongings which he packed into the holdall. He then went to the washroom to freshen up and shave, still with his wig and clear-lensed spectacles on.

The fugitive Green bought a ticket for the 7.30am southbound train, and sat down nervously to wait for it's departure.

Bill Harris was also up early, and looked out of his guesthouse window to see that the weather had improved, although there was still drizzle falling and a fresh breeze was moving the trees. Telephone lines had been down the night before, and he hadn't been able to contact London about the new developments concerning Green and the CIA agent. Harris could now only go straight to the Director General of the MI5, or to the Home Secretary himself. The latter option seemed improbable for a man of his modest rank, so he decided to speak to the office-bound Ian Burton as soon as possible, to sound him out on the whereabouts of Duncan Hyde the DG.

"I want you to tell him to expect an urgent and highly confidential call from me, as soon as you can rig up a hotline Ian ", he said to the young office administrator.

"I'm on to it right away Sir. How is the weather down there in the sticks?, said Burton, "I heard on the wireless that the West Country has had its worst storms for over fifty years".

"I wouldn't be at all surprised, replied his chief, " a bit better today though".

As he put the phone down, Harris thought about the other storm that was soon to break in London, in both MI5 and government circles.

Green's train left Bath on time, and the latest news was that the line was now clear all the way through to Bournemouth, not that he intended going that far. Once again, the Midsomer Hollow area of Somerset was going to be the scene of the action, but this time where the last part of the drama would be played out.

The disguised Operations Chief of MI5 alighted the train, and was met with the sight of two uniformed police constables, one each patrolling the up and down platforms. Green had no doubt that his disguise would fool these country bobbies, but one of them was starting to approach him anyway. The real problem facing him though was that he couldn't carry on with what he planned with the police around, and he didn't really want to come back here when it was dark.

Once again he would brazen it out, and so started to walk towards the small carpark over by the large engine shed. The constable seemed to have lost interest in him, so Green walked towards the three vehicles standing there. A dark green Austin 16 had its key left in the ignition, its owner probably gone to meet one of the arriving passengers. Without hesitating, Green made his fatal mistake, slid into the drivers seat and pulled away.

Just as he was approaching the exit gate a voice shouted out, "Oi, come back here, that's my car!"

The police quickly saw what had happened and ran towards the gate, but Green was quicker. Should he turn left under the railway bridge and drive towards the centre of the town , or right up the hill? He turned right, and then left into Charlton Road which was a long avenue lined with residential properties and a couple of small shops. Before he had reached the end of the road though, he heard a police patrol with its bells ringing as he approached the crossroads. They hadn't wasted much time these country bobbies, and all local areas were obviously on the look out for him or for anything suspicious. "Well, he thought,"they must have had their car nearby so I can only try to lose them".

The London man though wasn't familiar with Somerset country lanes, and this was exactly what he encountered when he decided to drive straight ahead at the junction. Immediately he found himself on a lane lined with high hedges and poor visibility, with room for vehicles in one direction in some places. He passed a couple of gateways leading into fields, where one vehicle would have to stop to let others pass. Not today though, all the entrances to the fields were very muddy and sodden, and the last thing he wanted was to get bogged down.

After a hurried breakfast, Harris and Cartwright were driven to Bath police station and were greeted with the news that the stolen van had been found.

"The owner of some garage premises saw that the lock on one of them had been tampered with, recounted the desk sergeant, "and someone has obviously spent the night there in that Bedford".

"Good work sergeant, replied the secret service man, "give it a good going over, but keep this quiet. Don't even tell the American if he comes back here".

Tim Cartwright looked at his boss, and Harris said, "We need to know a bit more about Mr Dodd Tim, and exactly how and where he got this van and how much he knew about Green's movements. If the CIA have already contacted London about their investigations and surveillance of our MI5 Field Operations Chief, then I should have been told. If they haven't told them, then I will have Dodd arrested by Scotland Yard and he can explain everything to them".

Ian Green was lucky not to have met any other cars or farm tractors, and so far had driven the big Austin round the lanes without problem. Round a bend he could see a wider lane leading off to the right, but as he slowed he saw a sign blown over that said "Road Closed – Fallen Tree".
Without hesitating, he turned right and drove about fifty yards, then got out the car and ran back to put the sign back up at the entrance to the lane.

Listening before getting back in the stolen car, he could still hear police bells ringing, probably from more than one patrol car. The weather was murky and cold, and Green suddenly felt very lonely with the tall hedges pressing in on him. His chances looked bleak to say the least.

Just after nine that morning, Ian Burton put through a call to Bill Harris on a private line.

"I have Mr Hyde here for you Mr Harris", said Burton, then left the office and the phone in the hands of the Director General of MI5.

"Good Morning Harris, Hyde shouted down the line in his loud, but friendly voice, "I have some idea of what you are presumably going to tell me. The Americans have wired to say that they have been surveilling Ian, and that their man has told you something about the matter. I will just say that it hasn't come as a complete surprise to me, but what *is* a surprise is that this Gib document business could be part of his clandestine activities. He must be found at all costs Bill. You and Cartwright do the police work, and I promise to fill you in on everything later. It was bad enough for an individual to blackmail us with that document, but imagine what the Russians could do with it"

"I understand completely Sir, and we will do our utmost, replied Harris, but do I cooperate with the American?"

"No, tell him nothing, he may be their man in the field, but he has done his job. This is our beat now".

Harris had only met Duncan Hyde on a couple of occasions at official functions, but he felt that he had liked him. Hyde had also called him by his first name!

"Let's go and see this lock-up", said Harris, and stepped outside into what was now a decidedly foggy morning. Harris didn't like fog much as the "floaters" before his eyes were more pronounced against a white background! When he was younger, he was afraid to tell anyone about these squiggly smudges and lights that danced around his vision, and thought that he may one day go blind! He was assured though that they were harmless and that lots of people have them, something about particles getting detached and floating around in the eye fluid....

The two detectives never got to the scene of the discarded van though, the radio in the patrol car was telling them to proceed to Whiteway Lane where a crashed Austin 16 had been found. The police driver more or less knew his way around the county, and they were soon speeding south into the Somerset countryside. Headquarters were able to give the driver more precise directions, and they were able to say that the fire brigade and an ambulance had been sent.
When the MI5 reached the area, the lanes were chock a block with vehicles, and a constable was trying to restore some order. He saluted Harris as the patrol car pulled up alongside him, and the detective rolled down his window.

"Fill me in quickly constable", he said.

"From what I know Sir, a farmer heard a car horn jammed on, and then saw smoke rising above the hedges. He drove his tractor towards it and found a car crashed into a large tree that was down across the road".

"And the driver?", asked Harris.

"Still inside the car Sir, as far as I know. Someone disconnected the horn and presumably the firemen have put out the fire".

The police driver was instructed to carry on as far as he could, then Harris and Cartwright got out and walked the rest of the way to the crash scene where the ambulance men were just carrying someone to their vehicle on a stretcher.

"How is he?", asked Bill Harris.

"Alive, but barely", replied the St John man.

Bill Harris went closer, and saw instantly that the dying driver was indeed his boss Ian Green.

"I am going with you to the hospital, Harris said to the ambulance men, "Tim, you take statements with the local police and find out all you can".

The ambulance sped off , and Harris found himself going back to Bath once again.

"How badly hurt is he?", he asked the assistant.

"Bad Sir, we think he has head injuries. He hit the windscreen and was half hanging out. Lucky really that he was pressing down on the car horn, otherwise he might not have been found for hours round those lanes", replied the ambulance man.

Harris knew the man was critical, and that once inside the hospital wouldn't get the chance to try to talk to him, so he moved closer.

"Ian, Ian can you hear me? It's Bill Harris", he said softly to the other, close to his ear.

The ambulance man looked at Harris doubtfully, so he took out his identity card and showed it to the assistant which satisfied him that the stranger was a police officer.

Green stirred, and Harris told him to take it easy and that they would soon reach the hospital. "What were you doing Ian? Did you find the document?", Harris tried again.

The injured man tried to speak, and Harris moved closer.

"Bill...I'm, I'm sorry", he whispered.

"Never mind now Ian, I understand, but did you find the document?"

Green was struggling now to mouth some words. "Bill...Bill, I couldn't get to the....." his voice trailed off.

"Couldn't get to what Ian?", encouraged Harris.

"The....the pill....".

These were the last words he spoke, and when the ambulance arrived at St Margaret's Hospital, Ian Green was dead.

After the body had been delivered to the hospital mortuary, Harris approached the ambulance assistant and asked him, "Did you hear what he said before he died?"

"Yes Sir, sounded like he couldn't get to the pill, whatever that means", replied the other, a little puzzled.

"Hmmm, replied Harris thoughtfully, "yes, thank you for everything".

Bill Harris asked to see the hospital's head supervisor, and after showing his credentials was taken to the see the surgeon who would be making the autopsy on the dead man.

"This is Doctor Bernard Kirk,Mr Harris, said the supervisor. "Dr Kirk, this is Detective Harris from the police".

The two men thanked the supervisor, and she went on her way.

Kirk was a short, portly man in his late fifties. Obviously very experienced at his job, he had been an Army Surgeon in both world wars. He held out his hand and said, "I usually carry out the duties as police surgeon and coroner... Inspector Harris was it?"

Bill Harris smiled and replied that he was secret service.

Suitably impressed, the doctor asked how he could help, apart from in the obvious way.

"This is to be kept strictly secret doctor, he said, "but I would particulary like you to test for any poisons in the body".

"Such as?", replied the surgeon.

"Cyanide, for instance?" said the detective.

"Was this not simply a road accident then?" asked the doctor.

"Most probably yes, but please also search the usual places for a hidden capsule".

"Inside his mouth? said Kirk, "yes of course, will you stay while I do the autopsy"

"Yes I would like to, replied Harris, "but first can we strip him off and give his clothes a minute check over?"

An hour and a half later, the doctor concluded that death was due to serious head injuries caused by a road accident, throwing the deceased through the windscreen of the car when he collided with something in the road. There were no signs of poisons or drugs in the body, and there were no concealed poison capsules in hollow teeth, nor about the body or in his clothing. Harris digested these findings, and thanked the doctor as he left to go back to where his assistant Cartwright was.

Over lunch the two MI5 men pondered over their former chief's death, and tried to figure out what his last words meant.

"He couldn't get to the pill, repeated Tim Cartwright, "could he have said the hill, and not the pill?"

"It sounded exactly like pill Tim, and the ambulance man thought the same", replied his boss.

"The local police think it strange that Green drove into that fallen tree. I mean, he came round a bend, but why drive at it at such speed?", remarked Cartwright.

"Because he was being followed, and wanted to get away? Or is that too easy Tim?, said Harris.

"Well yes it is Sir, replied Cartwright "because when the farmer heard the noise from the scene, he found the *road closed* sign across the entrance to the lane. Now, why would he drive into the lane, put the sign back up, and then drive at speed down the lane knowing that there was a dangerous fallen tree somewhere?"

"What do you mean *put the sign back up* Tim? Did he move it out of the way, or wasn't it ever there?".

"The farmer thinks he can remember the sign being blown over earlier. The wind was very strong remember, and also one side of the sign was covered in mud indicating that it had been laid down or blown over", continued the junior detective.

Harris was pondering all this, and lit a cigarette. "You know Tim, my theory is that Ian knew he had no chance and decided to end it all. For some reason he couldn't swallow a cyanide pill, so killed himself by crashing instead".

"Suicide then?", asked Cartwright.

Bill Harris spoke again with Duncan Hyde on a private line, and told him of Green's death. Hyde simply said, "Come back to London immediately Harris, call me as soon as you arrive".

CHAPTER 23

The weather had settled down now, and trains were running normally again. Harris was on a late afternoon express to Paddington, and by 9pm was sat in the office of Duncan Hyde, the Director General of MI5.

"Have you eaten yet Harris?", he asked the other.

"No Sir, only a sandwich on the train".

"I will treat you at my club later, so let us get this over with. What is your opinion of Green's death?"

"Well Sir, started the detective, "either he put the road closed sign up to cover the fact that he had driven up the lane, and then drove too fast to miss the fallen tree. You know, maybe simply forgotting about it in his haste"

"Or?", asked Hyde.

"Or else he deliberately tried to kill himself", replied Harris.

"But why bother to put the sign back up, what was the point?"

"I've checked Sir, and found out that Ian Green had a sizeable insurance policy out on his life. If suicide were found to be the cause of death, then of course there would be no pay out", explained Harris.

"Presumably his wife would be the beneficiary, but wasn't their marriage on the rocks Harris?"

"Yes Sir, replied the agent, "they were living apart, but my guess is that once Green knew he had no chance, he gambled on the life insurance paying off his debts".

"The hell it will", exploded the up to now placid Hyde. I will personally make sure that no insurance money is paid out, suicide or no suicide".

"You said you weren't surprised that this American organisation, the CIA were investigating Ian", asked Harris.

"Look Bill, replied the chief, the top echelons knew that secrets were being leaked, and so did the CIA. It was fairly obvious that it was a Brit, so everyone, you and Cartwright included were under suspicion".

Harris began to protest, but Hyde cut him off.

"The only way to find out the identity of the traitor was for an independent body to investigate, that's why this Dodd fellow was here, and it was he who stumbled onto Ian, although to your credit you already had him marked down. What none of us knew though was that this Gibraltar document business was involved. We had been blaming the Spanish Republic, or someone, but it was the Soviets behind the scheme all the time".

Bill Harris was drinking all this in, and then took a bold step, "I think it's about time I was briefed fully about the whole affair Sir".

To his surprise Hyde agreed. "You have done well Bill, even though the document hasn't been found. I am recommending you to take over Green's vacancy as Senior Field Operations Chief. As soon as the Home Secretary gives his ok, I will fill you in. In the meantime, what do you think of our chances of recovering the document?"

"Slim Sir, to be honest", he replied.

"Be honest again Bill, asked Hyde, "do you think he managed to give the document to the Russians, and then decided to kill himself?"

Harris though long before answering in the negative.

"Apparently, the CIA man thinks Green knew more or less where to find it after his accomplice had deceived him, and left a cryptic note to that effect in that left luggage box".

"Harris then asked the big, big question, "Why do the Russians want the document Sir, and how dangerous is it to us?"

"Let's go to dinner, I will tell you what I think"

Duncan Hyde's Mayfair club had lost none of its pre war quality and reputation, and the two MI5 men had an excellent meal. The waiter brough them two large brandies, then fetched the humified cigar box. Both men made their selection, and waited while the ends were cut and the bands taken off, Hyde holding the end of his a long time under the match while eyeing his colleague.

Blowing his first puff of smoke in the air, he said to Harris, "Bill, you seem a humane type person, maybe you could sympathise with Green. You know, he had marital problems, stress from work, got into gambling debts over his head. Would you have any qualms about stepping into a dead man's shoes, even if he was tempted to go astray".

"Well, replied Harris, "with respect Sir I haven't stepped into them yet!"

"But you do understand possibly how he got himself into a mess, and why he did what he did?".

Bill Harris was no fool, and knew Hyde was sizing him up, but nevertheless he answered totally honestly.

"No Sir I'm afraid I don't. Oh, men have always got themselves into debt through gambling or women, and they always will, but I can't understand anyone betraying their country".

"To the Russians especially?", prompted his boss.

"To the Russians, or anyone else", he replied emphatically.

Hyde presisted, "What would you have done in my place if Green hadn't died and had been arrested".

"I would see him hanged Sir, as a traitor, as I'm sure you would too"

Hyde smiled and ordered two more brandies, "You bet your life I would, in my opinion even hanging would have been too good for him, and as I said, there will be no insurance pay out. His death will no doubt be recorded as by traffic accident, but his insurance company will be only too glad to follow our official line, regardless of whether it was suicide or not".

Hyde was satisfied now that he could devulge more to his companion, and took a sip of his brandy.

"You see Harris, the Russians were behind everything, the killing of General Franco's envoy to Britain, that Juan Galvez Ruiz, the placing of Juan Pardo as his double, the blackmailing of the Spanish woman Arancha, the lot".

"Arancha was an unwilling accomplice?", asked the surprised detective.

"We think so yes, but our investigations, or rather yours, smiled Hyde, "haven't been concluded yet".

"So what are the Russians motives Sir?" asked Harris.

Duncan Hyde pulled hard on his cigar, and sent a blue plume of smoke towards the ceiling. Looking at the man, Harris couldn't help wondering how long it would be before his chief would receive a knighthood. He had seen the way that he could turn from affable boss to cold hearted executioner, and Harris had no doubt of the pressure that the MI5 head was under. Success would be rewarded, but failure could be costly for everyone, from the government down.

"The answer to your question in broad terms, continued Hyde, "is a foothold in Western Europe. Oh, I know they have part of Berlin, but the Americans will never allow them to progress beyond there. Stalin is no fool, and he has got some of his territories through trickery, but he has always put importance on signed declarations and agreements, even if his interpretation of them are different to others".

"But how will an agreement giving Gibraltar back to Spain, signed by the British Government, help him?", asked Harris.

"We can only speculate of course, replied the MI5 chief, "but the main theory we are working on is as follows. Stalin once again appeals to the Western Powers that General Franco is the last vestige of facism in Europe, and that his regime should be dismantled and replaced with democracy. The United States and Britain will obviously turn this down, not only as they will see it as an attempt by Stalin to perhaps set up a partitioned Spain as a second Berlin, but also because they see General Franco's regime as no danger to the world compared with the spread of communism".

"Stalin must have refugees from the Spanish Republic working for him Sir, that's clear from how he was in the know about Franco's envoy etc", put it Harris.

"That's a good point. We think he has a very good spy network operating in mainland Spain and France", replied Hyde.

"And the Gib document Sir?", prompted Harris.

"As I said, his boss continued, "we can only surmise, but supposing Stalin's demands are turned down by the western alliances, he could then through private diplomatic channels threaten the British government with the document. Atlee wouldn't be able to deny its existence, and Stalin knows that the US frown upon our overseas territories, so his warped mind might possibly think that Truman would be in favour of us losing sole control of Gibraltar".

"So Stalin would blackmail Britain into accepting, or even suggesting a partioned Gibraltar, said Harris warming to the theory, "and from there on he would continue working away to install a Spanish communist republic".

"Precisely Bill", replied Hyde, back on first name terms! "It would place us in a big dilemma. Truman of course would fight it, but at the end of the day Gib belongs to us and we would have the final say. It would be a choice of giving it back to Spain altogether, or sharing it with our allies".

"It could even cause another war, suggested Harris, "this time between the West and the Soviet Union over Spain".

"Another facet of Stalin's warped thinking, said Hyde, "is that Atlee as a socialist may be in favour of getting rid of Franco. Churchill is gone now, and many union workers fought for the republic in the Spanish Civil War".

"Do you see that as a possibility Sir?", asked Harris.

"Not a chance, was his superior's reply, "Atlee may be a socialist, but he shares Churchill and Truman's fear of Stalin's intentions of global communism. Spain is still a poor and devastated country after their civil war, and they need western help. Franco is no Hitler or Mussolini, he is clever and saw the writing on the wall for the Nazis and kept Hitler at bay. Spain will be an important bastion against communism, that's why the Americans are offering them help, and wily Franco is milking everything he can for his country".

Harris had taken most of this in, but as Hyde as remarked, it was all surmise at this stage. It was time to ask his big question. "Suppose the Russians did not get hold of the Gib document, but pretend that they had, and proceed with their blackmail?"

"I don't go for that Harris, they know of the documents content more or less, but maybe not of its exact wording. Proof of possession would be needed anyway", Hyde replied.

Harris had another thought, "This CIA chap told us that his people have an agent, presumably in Moscow, who tipped them off about a British leak".

"Yes, replied Hyde, "that is what this Crawford Dodd told you?"

"Yes Sir, he did. So why don't we get him to arrange for the Russians to be told about the document's loss. Their plant could tell them that all our searches have been fruitless, and that we are dropping the matter", suggested Harris.

Hyde thought about this, and drank off the remainder of his cognac. "That's good Bill, very good. If Green managed to give them the document, then we should hear from them quite soon I would think. Otherwise, they will either believe that we are bluffing, or they really have recovered the agreement".

"Which amounts to the same thing really, and keeps them off our backs", remarked Harris.

"Not quite the same thing, replied Hyde. If they feel we are bluffing and that the document has really not been found, then they probably have people here who will continue searching. On the other hand, we cannot tell Stalin that we have found the stolen document, as he could then go public and ask us to make an official statement about its content".

"How do we go about it then Sir? asked Harris, "Tim Cartwright can find out if Dodd is still in the Bath area".

"No Bill, I will contact the CIA myself, and they will have to advise us. If they involve Dodd, then that will be their decision".

The meeting broke up, and the proposal was put to the CIA who happily accepted. Their agent filtered the news through to Moscow that a highly secret document damaging to the British Goverment had been stolen, but that all efforts in finding it had now been abandoned.
All everyone could now do was to sit and wait for any developments.

A week passed, then a month. Finally, after three months had gone by with no news from the Russians, Bill Harris the new Field Operations Chief was called once again before his superior Duncan Hyde, but this time the Home Secretary himself was also present at the meeting.

"So, gentlemen, started the cabinet minister, "after three months, what are your views".

Harris spoke, "In my view Home Secretary, the danger is past as regards the Soviets. The document could still well be found yet, and I have kept our man Cartwright stationed in the West Country to keep his ear to the ground and to follow up any leads".

The Home Secretary fumed, "Damn it man, that paper must be somewhere. Why don't you turn that monastery and school upside down. I don't trust those people".

Duncan Hyde smiled inwardly at the minister's presumed anti Rome sentiments and said, "I don't think that would be practical Sir, Downbury have been very helpful with our enquiries, and as their Abbot said, if the document was hidden on their premises, it would be as safe there as anywhere else".

Tim Cartwright for one didn't mind having to stay in Somerset a while longer, his friendship with Marjorie Knight the Methodist Minister was flourishing. The couple would marry two years later, but not before Tim had given up his job with the secret service. Marjorie never insisted on this, but Tim had seen enough violence in his short life and the couple eventually bought a smallholding in the Somerset countryside.

Bill Harris was Tim's best man at his wedding, and many years later he would recall the conversation the two had while popping out of the crowded reception for a smoke. Cartwright had asked his old boss if Crawford Dodd was still around, but Harris told him that as far as he knew he had returned to the States. "He was positive that Ian Green knew where Tanner had hidden the document you know Bill", he remarked.

"Because of the cryptic note he left him at the railway station? What did it say again?", asked Harris.

"Well, he wrote that he had taken all the risks but needed more guarantees from Green, and then said that the paper was safe and shock free".

"And what did Dodd make of that Tim?", he asked again.

"Naturally he didn't think it provided a clue to the document's whereabouts as such, only that it signified that it was in a safe place and therefore wasn't going to shock anyone", replied Cartwright.

"So did he advise you that you were wasting your time to be still searching for it?".

"He didn't say that no, but when we had to finally give up our search he had an even bigger grin on his face than usual!"

Bill Harris was Field Operations Chief of MI5 until he retired in 1965, but hardly a day went by without him thinking of the Somerset affair.

Duncan Hyde would retire with a knighthood!

PART TWO – The Spanish Connection

Extremadura in South West Spain, and Somerset in South West England have more than a few similarities. Both are rural, agricultural areas, and both have smaller nations lying to their western borders in Portugal and Wales. Unlike the eight provinces of Andalucia, Extremadura has only two, Badajoz and Caceres, although Badajoz is singularly Spain's largest. Like Bath in Somerset, Badajoz has much Roman history, and the city of Merida has the largest collection of Roman relics in Europe, including an amphitheatre. In Ridley Scott's 2000 film Gladiator, Russell Crowe's character Maximus supposedly came from Merida. Given the name for its extremes in temperature, Extremadura produces some of Spain's best hams – the pata negra from pigs fed on the local acorns.

CHAPTER 24

Badajoz is a sprawling land of olive trees and grape vines, of cork trees and typical Spanish pueblos. Many of these pueblos and cities saw heavy fighting during the civil war, and after the Nationalists victory, the rich landowners and farmers continued to be the privileged class. Defeated Republicans who survived the war and it's aftermath of *purges*, either left the country, or kept their opinions to themselves if they wanted to work and feed their families.

During General Franco's regime, the Roman Catholic Church and the Spanish state were inseperable, and it was to a landowning family in Badajoz that the baby daughter of Arancha Gomez Ruiz was sent in 1946. Arancha herself was born in Catalonia in 1922, and during the siege of Barcelona in the Civil War both of her parents were killed in the bombing of that city. The family were anarchists, and as Barcelona's capitulation became certain, the 16 year old Arancha was forced to trust someone. That someone was the young communist Juan Pardo. Pardo had been a leader in the republican militia, but Moscow's influence was growing and he was intelligent. The Russians saw potential in him, and sent him to Moscow to receive training and political indoctrination. Over 600.000 Spanish refugees took refuge in the South of France, and Arancha was among the first of the women, children and old people to be admitted into a French camp. The frontier was temporarily closed, but negotiations with the French government opened it just in time to receive the Republican soldiers fleeing from Franco's forces.

Pardo and Arancha met on a couple of brief occasions, but with the outbreak of World War Two the Spanish evacuees found themselves in another plight. The French government gave men between the ages of eighteen and forty eight the following four options: to work in French industry or Argriculture,to help build fortifications against the Nazis, to sign up for five years with the Foreign Legion, or to join a regiment of foreigners fighting alongside the regular French army. Juan Pardo chose the second of these options, but soon both he and Arancha had joined the French Resistance as Maquiards

Pardo's links with Soviet Russia were seemingly severed when Hitler declared war on them in 1942, but he hadn't been forgotten by them, as he would find out three years later.

In May 1945 the victorious Soviets were looking to extend their influence not only in Japan and the Far East, but also in Western Europe. Men like Pardo could be useful to them, and the

Soviet secret police had found out something that could be persuasive as regards to the Spaniard.

Juan Pardo was a true *rebel without a cause*. Born into a well to do family in Extremadura, he grew to resent being the second son and became very different to his older brother Francisco. *Paco* was very right wing and religious, and worked very hard supervising his father's estate. The family owned acres of land which produced grapes, olives and wheat amongst other things, but Juan was a black sheep to his father, and was never interested in working in the campo. His political leanings were to the left, and before the Civil War had broken out, he had moved to Barcelona where he found work in a factory, and started attending trades union and anarchist meetings.

Not long after Pardo had left his pueblo in Extremadura, the body of a guardia civil officer had been found. The agent had been missing for several days, and had been knifed to death. It seems that he had caught and tried to arrest a group of youngsters who were vandalising a church, and many villagers tied the crime to the fled Juan Pardo. Pardo's parents were obviously shamed over these rumours, but they kept their dignity and no blame was officially attached to them. Paco joined the Falange movement, but the family fervently hoped that brother would never have to fight against brother.

During the Second World War when Hitler was still trying to get Franco to enter on his side, Paco Pardo decided to join the División Azul, the Spanish Blue Division of volunteers who fought bravely against the Russians at Stalingrad. Pardo's father did not want his son to leave for war a second time, but it seemed as though Paco was trying to make up for his brother's desertion of his family and background.

Paco was among the hundreds of thousands of Russian prisoners of war, and many of the Spanish ones didn't survive the Siberian concentration camps.

One day, a sharp eyed official saw Pardo's surname and started investigating...

Juan Pardo was found in France by a Soviet contact, and was told that a flight to Berlin had been arranged for him to meet his *old comrades..* A hint was also dropped to him that something important had been found out about Juan's brother Paco.

Officials from the NKGB lavished food and good wines on Pardo, asked him about his late career, and questioned him about his political views. Juan had lost none of his old fire, and his outspoken views on General Franco's regime warmed the hearts of his Soviet interrogators.
The Spaniard was told that they had him in mind to become part of their eyes and ears in France, but that he was to groom someone else, a woman, to be planted in Britain.

Pardo accepted the Russians offer gladly, but then asked the secret policemen what they knew about his brother.

"What do you know about him comrade Pardo?", asked one of the NKGB men.

"I haven't seem him, or heard anything about him since I left home nine years ago", he replied.

"Ah yes, you left early in 1936. Perhaps you saw the writing on the wall comrade, and our friends in Barcelona saw something in you. Tell me, he continued, "what do you feel for your brother, and for your family?"

"I wouldn't want any harm to come to them of course, but I can never go back home. I don't hate them but...."

"They may hate you?", suggested the Russian.

"I suppose so, yes", he admitted

"Well we understand comrade, after all you are Spanish, and you want the best for your country and your people. In fact comrade Pardo, your brother fought against us with a fascist division at Stalingrad, but the Motherland was glorious and your brave brother is now in a prisoner of war camp in Siberia".

Pardo went silent as he took all this in. "Yes, that would sound like Paco, he replied, "but is he alright. Is he alive".

The NKGB men assured him that his brother was alive, but that many thousands of fascist prisoners had died. "We don't have the food and medicines to give them, he lied, "and many have committed suicide".

"How long will they be prisoners?, asked the Spaniard.

"No one knows, that is up to Secretary Stalin, but possibly he thinks ten years may be sufficient punishment".

"Well the fascist bastards deserve it, snarled Pardo, "even my brother. If you want to let him go home, then do so, but it won't make any difference to me".

Even the unscrupulous NKGB man thought Pardo at that moment a callous man.

The Russians had already set up quite a reasonable network of agents in France, handpicked from likely Spanish republican exiles. Stalin wasn't satisfied with a trade embargo against Spain, he wanted the Allies to destroy the Franco regime. Pardo was given a leading role, and his first task was to set Arancha up in the UK. She was fixed up as a hospital auxiliary , but Pardo always told her that one day the Spanish Republic would be reinstated, and that she would have a part to play. "Franco will be driven from Spain by our allies, he told her, "and you will be able to revenge the death of your parents." Arancha would meet rich and influential people in London, that was her duty, and she would be planted there as a sort of mole, waiting until she was contacted for an important assignment. First though she had to improve her English, and then wait until *they* called her .

As luck would have it Pardo and Arancha suffered a catastrophe, for a few weeks after she arrived in England she found out that she was pregnant. Juan panicked, presumably he was the father, but he knew that his Russian masters would be displeased. They must not know about it, so he tried to persuade Arancha to have an abortion. Arancha refused however, and the couple rowed. Arancha was a tough individual who had shown her grit both in Barcelona and in occupied France, but she would not allow any backstreet doctor to touch her. Anyway, she was working in a hospital and could ask the authorities for help.

Arancha was a popular girl at work, the young doctors doted after her, and everyone felt sympathy for her plight. She made things quite clear that although she wanted the baby to be born, she couldn't keep it, and that he or she were to be taken away for adoption to a good family immediately. Juan Pardo meanwhile was visited again by a senior NKGB man, and he feared that plans were being hatched for Arancha and himself. Instead, the official told him that his brother Paco had been released from the prisoner of war camp in Siberia, and papers were being prepared for his early return to Spain.

"We hope you appreciate this gesture from Secretary Stalin comrade, he said ironically, "even if you don't show it".

Juan thanked the man, and a plan was hatching in his head. He had no idea though of the plan that the Russians were hatching for him, or to the extent of their knowledge of British/Hispano affairs.

CHAPTER 25

Arancha and Juan exchanged letters frequently, and it was agreed that the baby be adopted to a family in Spain. This would be no easy thing though, Spain weren't allies of Britain, and in any case the bureaucracy and red tape would be enormous.

The now seven months pregnant woman took her problem to her employers, and the hospital supervisors advised her that in their view the only people who could help were the Catholic church.

A Spanish speaking priest with experience of the country was located, namely the Abbot of Downbury, and he was found to be willing to act as a go-between provided that he was dealing with Nationalist Spain, and that a respectable Roman Catholic family would receive the child.

The Abbot also insisted on knowing Arancha's background, and also that of the father, if possible. He knew he would have problems with Spain accepting the child of an anarchist exile, but if the authorities there had an inkling that the father was also a suspected criminal, then not even the church could help.

At this point Juan Pardo wrote a letter to his parents. It was the first communication of any sort he had made to them since 1936, and he had to disguise it as arriving from someone else. He wrote that he had gone his own way as others had gone theirs, and that nothing could change that. Then, he broke the news that Paco would soon be home from Russia, and that he, Juan, had been involved in arranging this.

A few days later Pardo was summoned to East Berlin, and the Russian official who met him off the long train journey told him that his brother Paco was here, and that a meeting of the two had been arranged. Juan was immediately angry at this as he hadn't planned seeing his older brother in the flesh again, although he calmed down when reminded by the NKGB man that Secretary Stalin had great faith in him, and that this was just one little favour of the many that would be bestowed on both he and Arancha in the future.

The meeting was set for right where they were in the railway station, and in an hours time.

Juan was taken to the cafeteria and given a large meal, but he didn't have much appetite and was worried and nervous about meeting his brother face to face after all these years.

"Will I be able to speak to him alone", asked Pardo.

The Russian never answered straight away, then took the cigarette holder out of his mouth and smiled a smile that showed his gold teeth. Pardo had taken an instant dislike to the man, who replied, "Of course comrade, we will make sure that you will not be disturbed, but the meeting must be brief. Ten minutes maximum".

Juan Pardo nodded, and excused himself to the toilet. As he entered the lavatory he held the door slightly ajar, and looked back at his table. The Russian was calling someone over to him.

Juan went into a cubicle, got out a pencil and piece of paper, and started to write something. Pulling the flush, he returned to his place.

A waiting room had been put at the disposal of the brothers, and Juan stood up when two Russian soldiers brought Paco in. Paco was clean shaven but pale and drawn, and beside his brother looked thin and wasted.

The NKGB official said to the prisoner of war in excellent Spanish, "Paco, you have your brother here to thank for your release. Normally enemies of our Motherland are not treated so leniently", but if he was expecting thanks from the Spaniard he was disappointed. Pardo senior glared at him and said nothing.

"Well, recovered the Russian," we will leave the two of you alone for ten minutes, for Paco has a train to catch and has a long journey ahead of him". With that the three Russians left the waiting room. The two uniformed soldiers were really disguised Russian agents too, and the three of them went next door to hear what the brothers were saying to each other in the bugged room.

Juan was shy and nervous, and he could see that his older brother wasn't going to be the first to speak. "Do you know anything of our parents Paco?", he asked awkwardly.

"I could ask you the same thing *hermano*, at least you have been in a position to find out. Or have you been too busy working for these communist scum".

The Russian official Kolev stiffened when he heard this on his earphones, but carried on listening.

"We both chose our ways brother, replied Paco, "we were on different sides, but no one forced you to go and fight the Russians. Do you know how lucky you are to be still alive, let alone being freed?"

"You don't have to tell me, replied the older brother, and his face suddenly showed all his sorrow. "I have seen enough to last several lifetimes".

There was an awkward silence, then Juan broke it with the words, "When you get home, please tell our parents that I asked for them. Tell them that I am sorry. For you it is possible to go home, for me it is not. Impossible while that devil is allowed to rule Spain".

Paco seemed to soften at this, then asked, "Tell me brother, was it you who killed that Guardia Civil all those years ago?.

Juan want quiet, then looked his brother in the eye and said simply, "Yes".

If Juan were to ask his brother a favour in return, then he knew he would have to ask it while they were being frank with one another. There could be no glossing over who each of them were, and what each stood for.

Juan looked at his watch, and then at the door. He caught his brother's eye, and quickly passed the written note to him. Paco opened his mouth to speak, but the younger Pardo put his finger to his lips. Paco put the note in his pocket, and they both stood up as the Russians came back into the room, quite pleased with what they had heard.

"I never asked you if you were married brother, said Juan suddenly, "did you marry Pilar?"

"Yes, we got married *hermano*, in 1940 after the war".

"I am glad, replied his brother, "and children, do you have any children?".

"No children no, I left soon after, said Paco straightening up and looking Kolev in the eye, "to join the División Azul".

Kolev looked thunder but said nothing, and Paco Pardo was hustled out by the two *guards*. That was it, no handshakes no embraces, and no more words between the two brothers. Paco was taken to Checkpoint Charlie, handed over to the Americans, and within an hour was in a train on the first leg of his long journey back to Extremadura.

As soon as he had a chance, Paco got out the note that Juan had given him and read.

"Brother, must ask big favour in return. Please adopt our baby, you will be contacted".

Arancha's baby girl was taken away for adoption immediately after she was born. Although heartbroken, this was the way Arancha wanted it, and the way it had to be. She didn't even look at the girl or hold her, that would have been too much to bear, and would have made her change her mind about not keeping her. Arancha was assured that a good family had been found for the baby, and she left it for others to name the child. Juan decided not to tell her straight away that his brother and sister in law had adopted the baby, but instead gave her a buff coloured envelope to give to the adoption authorites which contained details of the family who would like to accept the baby girl. Arancha signed what papers she needed to, without reading them. Heartboken, she entered a period of depression that lasted three months, while all the time Juan was holding off his Russian employers who were keen for Arancha to be set up as a *host* in London.

The adoption process went through smoother than expected, with not too many questions asked. The Spanish authorities, keen to show that the regime was friendly to the Western Allies, kept the paperwork to the minimum, and the little girl was christened Pilar after Paco Pardo's wife. Ten months after Paco was reunited with his family, Pilar gave birth to a child of her own, another girl who the couple named Maria. It was the done thing during Franco's regime to name one of your daughters Maria, and the two sisters grew up together with love and security.

Pilar became a beautiful young lady, slim with long dark hair like her mother, but Maria was plainer and seemed to be less outgoing and sociable as her adopted sister. To an outsider, it looked like a repeat of the younger Pardo's jealousy of his older brother, but this time it was Paco's daughter who seemed the bitter one.

When she was eighteen years old, Pilar met and fell in love with a young medical student called Pablo. The couple married three years later and moved to Badajoz city. It was when Pilar reached eighteen, that Paco and his wife broke the news to her that they weren't her biological parents, and that she had been adopted. Pilar took the news well as she loved her adopted parents and sister, but when Paco and Maria were out of the house Pilar Senior would sometimes sit down with her adopted daughter and tell her titbits about her Uncle Juan. Pilar told her daughter never to mention these things to her father, but insinuated to her that she had been born in England, and that although adopted, she probably had the same family blood. This was rather confusing to the eighteen year old, but it somehow made her feel happier, and she vowed one day to find out more about her own past, and that of her real parents.

Maria meantime courted the son of a neighbouring landowner, and they were also married a year after Pilar. Pilar and Pablo's daughter Nuria was born in 1970, while the following year Maria gave her husband Manuel a baby son, whom they named Francisco after her father Paco.

Paco Pardo Senior survived his younger brother Juan by many years, and died aged 80. Paco's two grandchildren were the beneficiaries of his will, Nuria would inherit the house, and Paco junior his land. Of course, the children's parents would also enjoy the properties during their lifetimes.

Nuria and her husband Luis had a child of their own, a girl Victoria who was born in 1995. It seemed that this side of the family weren't to be blessed with sons, but the couple were delighted with their beautiful daughter.

The turn of the millennium brought cruel bad luck to Pilar. Pablo was never a strong, healthy type, and it was thought that he had contracted a virus from one of his patients that killed him at the early age of fifty six. No sooner had Pilar become accustomed to being a widow, when a tragedy even more cruel overtook her. Her daughter Nuria and son in law Luis were killed in a road accident in the North of Spain, but miraculously the six year old Victoria was unhurt.

Grandmother and granddaughter were good therapy for each other, and as the pain eased slightly as the years passed, the two became unseperable. Pilar decided to stay in her Madrid apartment, and it was in the capital that Victoria was brought up.

Trouble was brewing again for Pilar though. Her brother in law Manolo and nephew Paquito tended the land that Paquito had inherited from his grandfather, and it was an unwritten agreement that they lived in the family house. The campo was not the good business it had once been though, and ever since Spain had joined the European Union the small farmers had seen the demand and prices of their oil, wheat and grapes diminish. There was more competition now from Italy, France and other EUcountries, and the local wine and olive oil were sold to a cooperative each autumn so that they could get the best prices for the products when the market seemed right. This could mean that the farmers would have to wait a year or more before receiving payment.

Paco junior was now married himself with two children, and was struggling to make ends meet. He and his parents were beginning to think that they had had the thin end of the stick regarding the inheritance, and as families tend to, began plotting. Maria was the driving force behind the two men, and she felt that they would stay in their ruts for ever without her lead.

"My father left his house and land to his grandchildren, she said one day, "but you Paco are the only heir now, poor Nuria is dead, but we have nothing in writing to say that the house goes to her daughter Victoria. Anyway, they live in Madrid, and Pilar is not even our blood, she was adopted and I say we should look into this".

"Ask an *abogado*?", remarked her husband.

"Yes, we will find a good lawyer, and if we can prove our case he will make sure everything is in your name, and your children will inherit. If business is bad someone will buy the land, but at least you will a roof over your head, your own roof".

Her husband Manolo looked thoughtful and said, "Pilar has never bothered us before, her and her granddaughter have no interest in living here, they are city people".

"That's not the point, snapped Maria, "we must make things legal".

"Have you heard from her recently?", asked Manolo, looking at her sideways.

Maria didn't answer at first, but saw the two men eying her closely.

"Alright yes, I had a letter from Pilar yesterday, she and the girl want to come to stay for a few days", she uttered grudgingly.

A hush came over the room, which was broken by Maria saying, "She can't stay, we haven't got room. She can stay in the Hostel, in Bar Rosa".

Paco her son said, "There will be a row mother, you know that?".

"Yes, replied his mother, "there will be a row and a showdown, but we must be firm".

In Pilar's letter to her stepsister she gave Victoria's e mail address, and asked that if either Paco

or his children had internet they could reply much quicker that way. Paco and his wife Aurora had a daughter of fifteen named Paula, and a son Alejandro, who at seventeen was a year younger than Victoria. The two children had internet, so their parents and grandparents spent the evening devising the message they wished to be sent to Pilar and Victoria.
It ran:

"Dear Pilar, we hope that you and Victoria are well, and we would be both surprised and pleased to see you here in the pueblo. Unfortunately, we cannot put you up in the house as there are the six of us living here, but there is a very comfortable and reasonably priced hostel nearby. You would be welcome to share our meals, but we are a bit rough and ready, and there is not much room in the house. Please let us know if and when you are coming. Saludos Maria, Manolo, Paquito, Aurora, Alejandro y Paula".

The next morning Alejandro checked his incoming mail to find a reply from Victoria's address:

"Dear Sister, We will let you know when we have settled on a date to visit, and note your comments regarding accommodation. I should let you know at this stage, that it is Victoria's intention to put the house up for sale at some time in the future, and she would of course give yourselves first choice should you be interested in purchasing.
Un beso, Pilar y Victoria.

On seeing this, Manolo nodded knowingly, and Paco looked at his mother and said, "I told you so, my cousin thinks the house is hers".
Maria's face darkened, and Alejandro was instructed to reply to say that papers were being prepared to prove that the house belonged to Paco, and that after Nuria's death the will had no provision that her children would inherit. He was also told to remind Pilar that she had no blood ties with the family.
From that day on it was open war. Pilar reminded her stepsister that she and her family had been allowed to live in the house unmolested, even when Nuria was alive and living elsewhere, that they had never been charged rent, and that in return neither Nuria nor her daughter had ever received anything in return from the produce of their land.
Angry now, Maria let slip more than perhaps she should have, and retorted that Pilar's adoption by her parents was never legal, and that she was the child of *Rojos* and *criminales*.
No more e mails were exchanged after that day. Pilar felt crushed and depressed, but when she looked at her beautiful grandaughter her strength and will returned.
"What shall we do *abuela*?", Victoria asked her grandmother.
"We are going to fight those shameless ones Victoria. Somehow I am going to find out about the past, my past, and you can help me *cariño*, it's for your sake".
"But what if you find out something hurtful *abuela*, I don't want you to do that just for me", and started to cry.
"Don't cry *hija mia*, I want to find out the truth, I am old now and have nothing to lose, but you have your life in front of you and nobody is going to cheat you while I am still breathing".

Victoria was eighteen, and hoped to start university in the autumn. She was very intelligent and fluent in English and French, a bonus if she wished to follow a career in journalism which was her ambition. However, one of her hobbies had always been history, and she would spend hours surfing on the net and doing research projects.

"What year were you born *abuela*?, she had asked her grandmother the night before.

"1946", she was told.

"And you don't know where you were born exactly?"

Pilar answered in the negative, and the two women went to bed where they slept fitfully that night.

It was the holidays though, and Victoria was awake early the next morning. When her grandmother went to her room to call her for breakfast, she found the girl already on the computer. Victoria disliked laptops except when travelling, and had a good quality tower system in her room.

"*Buenos dias abuela*", she greeted Pilar.

"Good morning dear, she replied, "you are at work early! Come and have some breakfast".

Pilar sipped her coffee, and asked her grandaughter what she had been doing.

"Grandma, she replied, "I was searching on Spanish pages, and happened to see that a few years ago the Foreign Secretary was very interested in some confidential files that the British Government had released after 60 years. I was looking at the year 1948, and then I looked on English pages", continued the girl, not disclosing the fact that her search had been much more detailed and poignant than that.

"So?", asked her grandmother.

"There was a report of two Spanish nationals, a man and a woman, who were shot by British agents in that year somewhere in the West Country of England, related the girl excitedly, "apparently they were Russian spies, but the whole affair was very secret and even now not much information has been given out about it".

"But why would that interest our government now, and why would it interest us", asked Pilar.

"Well because the report mentioned something about Gibraltar, but what interested me was that the man's name was Pardo. My surname is Rodriguez after Papa, but Pardo after your side of the family grandmother...

CHAPTER 26

In August Extremadura is like a furnace, with temperatures sometimes over 40 degrees centigrade. Not usually humid like the coastal areas, at least it can get cooler in the night time. Streets are empty until at least nine o'clock in the evening when the people start to brave going outside. The Extremeños like most Spanish people, are creatures of habit, and when there is a fiesta or feria in the town they all flock to it. Otherwise, bars and restaurants have suffered the recent financial crisis and struggle to survive.

The house that Paco Pardo left to his grandaughter was a typical Spanish pueblo house, built nearly two hundred years ago. Its stone walls of half a metre thick keep the inside of the house cool in summer, and warm in winter. Modernised now, the passageway leading from the front door to the back used to be of cobblestones, and the mules for working in the fields would be led right through the house to the corral and stables at the rear. Bedrooms lead off to the left and right of the centre passageway, and the kitchen would be the last room with its back door leading onto the corral. Now, instead of housing mules, chickens and even pigs, the corral was made into a modern paved terrace and patio. If a family still farmed, their tractors and machinery could be kept there if a seperate entrance to the road had been made.

During the first years of the Civil War the Nationalist troops marched up from Málaga and Andalucia, defeating the Republicans town by town. Here, in the Pardo's pueblo there had been heavy fighting before the town was won for Franco, who by now was sole leader of the Right. Many Italian troops fought on the Nationalist side, and the mountains surrounding the town were strewn with bodies from both sides. Today, the mountains have been planted with pine trees, and there are green areas and official country walkways.

Victoria had only ever visited Badajoz once, when she was small, and had grown up in Madrid. She was slightly curious about going there again, although she now had a growing desire to find out all she could about her grandmother's past. She had a feeling that there was much to learn......

After Victoria had resumed surfing the net, her grandmother called her to ask if she wanted to go shopping with her.

"Not today *abuela*, if you don't mind", she called out. Victoria thought that she was on to something.

A book had been written about four years ago by someone called Breck, and apparently he was present when a woman was shot and killed in 1948 by Secret Service agents in a small English West Country village. With her pulse quickening, Victoria searched on.

Yes, the woman was a suspected spy, a Spaniard but working for the Russians. It seems as though the affair was kept secret for sixty years, but when information was released after that time Mr Breck wrote his memoirs on the strength of his being a physical witness to the events.

"I wonder if I can buy that book online, she thought, "have to find the title".

There it was "The Bloodstained Document" by Donald Breck, and it was available online as an e book.

"Grandmother, have you left yet, she shouted out, "can I use you credit card please!".

After forty eight hours the book had been read, and Victoria was now more convinced than ever that the affair was worth following up. She had the authors e mail address, and told her grandmother that she proposed writing to him.

"But it may have nothing at all to do with us dear, she replied, "there are many people called Pardo, and you can't just go around telling your business to strangers.

"I know *abuela*, replied Victoria, "but it recalls in the book how the authorities found out later that this woman had had a baby in 1946, and that it had been adopted by a family in Spain with the help of the Church. Apparently this village where she was killed has a large Roman Catholic Monastery and School".

Victoria saw the sad look on her grandmother's face and softened. "Listen grandma, if you want me to forget all about this I will. If we pursue it we might both get hurt, and find out something unpleasant".

After a few moments silence Victoria was about to turn off her pc,but her grandmother looked at her and said,

"Send the e mail *hija*. If he replies, then we will consider. I have been hurt before, so don't worry about me, if the truth is out there I want to know it".

Not only was Victoria very interested in finding out more about Mr Breck's book, she had genuinely liked reading it, and found what he had written about intriguing. It seemed as though the author wanted to bring the story up to date, and hinted that he had a theory as to what happened to the elusive Gibraltar document all those years ago. At least to break the ice, she could tell the author how much she enjoyed his book.

Pilar meanwhile, had spoken to a lawyer friend of her own, and he had asked her to call in to his Madrid office whenever possible. Antonio Guillen received her two mornings later.

"Have you found out anything Antonio? This is kind of you", she remarked, after the usual greetings were exchanged.

"I am glad to help you Pilar, he answered honestly, "did you know that there are plans to build an oil refinery in Extremadura", he asked.

"No, replied the woman lightly, "but it sounds a good idea to me if it brings work to the area, it certainly needs it".

"Yes, it does, agreed the abogado, "they have all the infrastructure there, a freight railway line to Sevilla, and the motorway that runs from there to Merida".

"I can't imagine the local farmers liking it very much though, she continued without much interest, "and don't those places give off pollution. I remember that one in La Linea smelt awful sometimes".

Antonio laughed and said, "Yes, we used to say it was the English in Gibraltar! Seriously though, these installations are much safer and more environmentally friendly now", he stressed the last three words with false importance. "And it is true that local landowners have fought these plans, although it looks as though the central government are going to give the go ahead at last", he went on.

Pilar thought all this very interesting, but wondered what it had to do with her. Antonio saw the look on her face and smiled. "You are wondering where this conversation is going aren't you ?, he asked. Then, suddenly the smile was gone from his face. "The fact is Pilar, that the refinery is earmarked to be built in Badajoz, namely in the area where your family live. Where you grew up". Pilar started to speak but Antonio put is hand up as if to say "be quiet, and listen".

"If, the refinery gets built Pilar it will be similar to when a motorway is constructed, but in a smaller way of course. The scheme will need land, and land always belongs to someone. In this case a good proportion of the land belongs to your family, and they will of course get compensation for having to give it up".

The lawyer now had Pilar's full attention as he went on."This could be a good thing for your nephew. The land is not as profitable as it was, everyone knows that, but the government would still have to pay considerable compensation, and because its the family's livelihood, they would probably end up better off than if they had sold the land".

"Yes I see that, remarked Pilar, "I know in the past farmers have been paid compensation if they have had to replace their old olive trees".

"And if they pull your house down?", asked the lawyer, looking at Pilar sideways.
"Yes, he followed up, "if you own a house on the land........"

"The compensation is more, obviously", remarked Pilar, now fully alert.

"Much more, answered her friend, "because the owner would be losing both his livelihood, and his home. There have been cases where the freeholder has even had a new house built for him. It isn´t exaggerating either to say that your nephew or his son could even be offered a job in the construction of the refinery, or actually working in it".

"Well that would be their good fortune, and I wouldn't deny them it, "replied Pilar, "but you have opened my eyes and they won't get what isn't legally theirs".

Victoria's English was good, and she sent her e mail off that evening:

"Dear Mr Breck, I have just finished reading your book "The Bloodstained Document" which I bought online, and found both entertaining and interesting. I must admit I came across your book as the result of searching the net for information regarding my grandmother's past. You see, my grandmother's paternal surname was Pardo, and she was born in England in 1946, before being adopted by a family in Extremadura, here in Spain. Of course, her background may have nothing at all to do with the characters in your book, and I apologise for my forwardness, but my grandmother needs to find out at least something of her past, as she is facing a court case where

she has to prove her identity.
Many thanks for your time,
Victoria Pardo Rodriguez
Madrid, Spain

CHAPTER 27

When Bill Breck retired as gamekeeper of Stanten House, his employers hoped that his son Donald would take over from him. Bill had been completely exonerated in the shooting of the Spanish woman fugitive in 1948. The MI5 officer testified at the time that his shot killed the girl first, and that Mr Breck opened fire with his shotgun only because he thought his son Donald's life was in danger. The father soon put the incident behind him, and was grateful that his son's kidnapping had not turned out worse for him.

The incident did affect Donald much more though. Barely nineteen years old at the time and on leave from his two years National Service, he and his father were sworn to keep quiet about what had happened on that fateful day in the country lane. Donald had of course, like Judy Wilson, been kidnapped by the fugitive Arancha Gomez Ruiz, and local people obviously knew that something serious had happened down that lane and that the police had shot and killed someone. The Brecks and others were told to say little, but if pressed, to state that an armed criminal was caught and shot in self defence by Scotland Yard officers.

Donald was an intelligent youngster, and was persuaded to stay on in the Army after his National Service was over, partly because he was good material, and partly because the authorities wanted him out of civvy street for a while. He duly signed on for twelve years, and when he was finally demobbed in 1962 it was as sergeant. His father Bill had sadly died the year before at the early age of fifty seven, and Donald proudly attended the funeral in uniform, noting that there were one or two smartly dressed strangers present.

After being stationed in Germany, Aden, Suez and other places, Donald took a while to settle down to village life again where his mother tried to spoil him as much as possible. The gamekeeper's position had been filled by Donald's younger brother Maurice, but Donald knew that he could take over the post if he wanted it. Instead, with the money he had saved he decided to work for himself, and bought a general stores and greengrocers in the village.

Over the years. Donald became a keen local historian and writer, and had several books published. His burning desire though was to be able to find out, and put to pen, those dramatic events that left such a mark on his life. Donald never married, and when his mother died he had just turned sixty.

Victoria was thrilled to see a message in her inmail the next morning from jjbreck4@gmail.com

Dear Victoria,
Many thanks for your mail, and kind words.
You probably realised from reading my book that my own family were involved in the incidents I wrote of. William Breck was my greatgrandfather, and Donald is my great uncle. Briefly, Donald is now eighty six, and unfortunately terminally ill. He is still very bright and lucid though, and was extremely interested when I showed him your e mail. I act as my great uncles *secretary* and general dogsbody! I don't know what that would be in Spanish!!
Perhaps you could tell me if your grandmother knows anything at all about her past, or that of her mother, and in what direction my research should take.
Best regards,
James Breck

Several emails passed between the two young people over the next few days. James was twenty five, and a junior in a law firm based in Bath. He wasn't seriously courting any girl, and had decided to enjoy his freedom for a while after studying his career for several years. He was devoted to his great uncle Donald though whom he visited daily, and the two shared an interest in local history and writing.

Donald knew that the Abbot of Downbury had assisted in the adoption of Arancha's baby daughter all those years ago, but he hadn't researched that part of the affair too deeply. James knew people at Downbury though, including some of the priests and teachers, and was put unofficially in touch with their librarian cum historian. With favours being discussed, including a pint or two of real ale in The Coach Arms, James found out what he was looking for, but wondered if it could be more than Victoria would want to hear.

His second line of enquiry though needed a bit more senority than he possessed, but his company secretary pulled strings, and managed to obtain what he wanted from Somerset House. It was with mixed feelings that he wrote to Victoria again that night.

Hi Victoria,
I now have answers to my enquiries regarding both the adoption process, and the birth certificate, and have completed most of the research that Donald may not have had previously. In

fact, except for the one missing piece, Donald would dearly love me to write an updated version of his book. Firstly though, I must ask if you and your grandmother really want to know all I have found out. It may not be well received. Also, I don't think this info
should be sent on an e mail, so could I phone you sometime?
Regards,
James

Victoria duly gave James her Madrid telephone number, and he messaged, telling her that he had been to Spain a few times, including Madrid on one occasion. He spoke and read a little Spanish, but said that he would speak to her in English. Victoria found herself getting impatient for 6pm, the time of James call to come around, but she also had feelings of trepidation. When the phone eventually rang she jumped, then for some reason felt herself blushing as she picked up the receiver.

"*Buenos tardes* Victoria!", he greeted her.

"*Buenos tardes* James *¿Que Tal?*",she answered delightedly.

"I am very well thank you, but we had better continue in English", he laughed.

"Please tell me what you can James, we want to know", replied the girl, looking round at Pilar who was by her side.

"Well, continued the Englishman, "to put it bluntly, I think my great-grandfather shot your great-grandmother, or at least jointly shot her". He waited for a reaction, but the end of the line was quiet, then...

"Go on please".

James went on, "Briefly, Downbury arranged your grandmother's adoption to Paco and Pilar Pardo, and it seems likely that Paco, your great-grandfather was released from a Siberian concentration camp because his estranged brother Juan was working for the Russians. We will never know exactly what happened, but the theory we worked on is that Juan made Arancha pregnant, but it was impossible for the couple to keep the baby. Maybe the Russians found out and forced the adoption, but this doesn't seem too likely".

"And you found out something about grandmother's birth certificate?, she asked breathlessly.

"Yes, replied James, "this is the best news for you. We have found out that a female baby was born on 2 February 1946 at the hospital where Arancha was working. The certificate shows the parents as Arancha Garcia Rodriguez and........"

"Paco Pardo", said Victoria quietly.

"No, replied James, "at least Juan didn't try to cheat on this".

"Then whose name is down as the father?", she asked with a breaking voice. Victoria held her grandmother's hand tightly and heard James say,"He put his own name down, Juan Pardo. Your great-grandfather may have been a Russian spy and an assassin, but your grandmother is related to her adopted family by blood, this makes it lawfully true".

The two women were very grateful for the information, and the phone conversation concluded with James telling them that no payment was owed to him, provided that they could come to mutual agreements concerning his use of parts of this information for his book.

Of course, he also told the girl, the birth certificate cannot be sent to you, nor can anyone else collect it. Pilar would have to collect it in person from Somerset House.

"This will help her a lot I'm sure", stated the girl, and James offered to contact and liaise with Pilar's lawyer in Madrid, promising to give him all the assistance he could.

"One more thing before we finish Victoria, he said, "if things reach that stage, Pilar's lawyer could push for DNA testing to be done on her and her stepsister. Or should we say on her cousin!"

Victoria felt hot, even though she was dressed in shorts and a small top and with the air conditioning on in the apartment. She looked thoughtfully out of the window at the sun-drenched street, and at the people sitting on the terrace bars sipping their deliciously tasting coffee. The municipal workers had been pruning the palm trees earlier, stopping at 10.30 for their morning breakfast of *bocadillo* brought from home and wrapped in tinfoil, then knocking off for lunch and siesta at 2pm. The cut branches were still littered on the pavement... they could be cleared up *mañana*.

The two young people looked forward to meeting each other in England in the near future, and Pilar was just as excited to be going there too. The information the two women had received was what they had expected to hear of course, but they could in no way be blamed for their ancestors crimes.

The Spanish Government, at the time headed by General Franco, naturally wasn't ignorant of all that had passed in the late forties, and the general found out that his envoy had been apprehended, killed and impersonated, and also that the returned Gibraltar Agreement document never found its way back to the British Government. This was in no way his fault, and he eventually got the United States and Western Powers help and recognition that he desired. Why should he care if the damning document was still in circulation somewhere.

The affair was filed away in the archives, but not forgotten. When the British released secret files in 2008, the then socialist Spanish Government took an interest in what had been made public about the Gibraltar affair, but took no action. This left-wing government seem best forgotten by the majority of Spaniards, who see them as failing to foresee the worst ever financial crisis that Spain, and most of the world have suffered. They seemed more intent on dragging up right-wing crimes from the Civil War, changing place and street names, and generally trying to rewrite history.

One of the Prime Minister's first acts was to pull his troops out of a Middle East War that Spain and her UN allies were involved in, and further annoyed the conservatives by making a young pregnant woman Defence Minister!

Gibraltar has an amazing population of thirty thousand people, but only a minority of these are British. This enclave is one of the few places in the world where Jews and Muslims live side by side in peace. Thousands of Spaniards cross the border every day to work in Gibraltar, mostly in catering, and their wages are higher than they would earn in their own country. Unemployment in Spain is the highest in the EU at around 25% , but this figure is much higher in most of the community of Andalucia.

A right-wing Spanish Government is always going to be tough over the Gibraltar problem, but they seem to be only able to wield the stick, and not dangle the carrot. Any new row or disagreement between Spain and Britain, inevitably means the Guardia Civil tighten up the border checks, and create long traffic tailbacks.

Donald Breck had been interested in keeping up with affairs in Gibraltar ever since he had written his book, and had, like many people, drawn his own conclusions and views on the prickly point of its ownership. He thought it unlikely that Spain would ever get Gibraltar back. Several referendums among its inhabitants had shown an overwhelming desire for it to stay British, and their wishes had to be respected. Perhaps the only solution would be to take the matter out of both countries hands, and for the EU to insist on some kind of gradual joint ownership of The Rock. "If that ever happened though, Donald thought,"it would be a very sad day for many".

CHAPTER 28

During the first week of September 2014, Pilar and Victoria were glad to be leaving behind the heat of Madrid for a couple of days as they boarded their flight from Barajas to Heathrow. James Breck was to be there to meet them, and he had arranged two nights stay for the women in a good London hotel. The flight was a morning one, so with the one hour time difference it would be nearly lunchtime when the couple arrived in London.

James was waiting in the arrivals lounge holding a board with the name Victoria Pardo, and the girl and her grandmother soon picked out the tall, handsome young man. He greeted them in Spanish, both with words and with the traditional light kiss on both cheeks, his lips barely touching their faces.

"We will get a taxi to your hotel ladies, so if you can just drop your luggage in your room, I will wait for you to come out and the driver will take us somewhere for lunch".

The two did as suggested, and giggled like schoolgirls as they went up to their room saying what a perfect English gentleman James was, "And *so* handsome", remarked the elder, laughing. James for his part, thought the pretty slim Victoria was very attractive, and that her grandmother could easily have been taken for her mother instead. James great-uncle Donald had recounted to him what a stunner Arancha had been, and told him that if he ever got to meet Pilar or Victoria, which he hoped he would, he almost would certainly see a resemblance.

When the two women came back to the taxi, James told the driver which restaurant he wanted him to drive to.

"After lunch we can go straight on to Somerset House, said James, "and then I thought perhaps tomorrow I can show you a few of the sights. We won't get to see too much though, he said thoughtfully, "you really need a week, or maybe a month!"

They laughed at this, and Victoria asked him what he thought of Spain, and Madrid in particular.

"I loved it, he answered, "except for your Spanish drivers. They don't do clutch control, and they don't seem to know what indicators are for!"

Victoria showed mock indignation and said, "And where are you taking us for lunch *Señor* Breck? I hope we aren't going to have fish and chips or baked beans!"

"Touche!", he laughed.

With Pilar's birth certificate secure in her possession, she and her granddaughter spent the night in and ate in their hotel.

The next day James took them to the usual sites, Buckingham Palace, Regents Park, and also a shopping trip to Harrods which is the nearest thing to Corte Ingles that Britain has. The three of them also visited the hospital where Arancha once worked and where she gave birth to her daughter, bringing tears to Pilar's eyes.

The next morning James saw them off on their early flight home, but first had several minutes alone with the girl.

Victoria thanked him once more for everything, and he told her that he hoped to see her again soon.

"Donald would like to see you so much,he said, "and it would be a fitting end for him if between us we could finish his story".

"Is he dying?", asked the girl.

"I think so, replied James, "but not just yet hopefully. He is eighty five after all".

"You mentioned that there was one piece missing, what did you mean?", asked Victoria.

"Well, Donald has a theory about what happened to the missing document in his book, and events are about to happen over the next few months that could prove him right", he answered her.

"So he, or you, could finish the book and solve the mystery. I think he would die happy then", she said.

James looked at her tenderly as she pulled a wisp of long dark hair from her eyes, and he knew that he must see her again.

The girl and her grandmother allowed themselves to be photographed by James, and with his mobile phone he took pictures of them together and seperate. "Donald will love to see them!", he explained.

When Pilar returned to Madrid with Victoria she took her birth certificate to Antonio Guillen the lawyer, and Guillen took copies, one of which he sent to the lawyer in Extremadura who was acting for Pilar's stepsister Maria. Antonio made it quite clear that Pilar's identity had been proven without doubt, both here and in the UK, and that he was starting procedures to draw up the *escritura* (deeds) of the Badajoz house in Victoria's name. He also hinted to the other lawyer that any opposition to this by his clients could instigate the request of certain *tests* to prove Pilar's relationship., and to show that she and Maria were actually first cousins. This seemed to do the trick as the *escritura* was drawn up, and nothing was heard from Maria or her family.

A week or two later Victoria sent a letter addressed to Maria and Manuel, telling them that she had no immediate plans to live in the house, or to sell it unless forced to, and that they and their family could stay there rent free for the time being.

This was a very generous action by the girl, and it was fully backed-up by her grandmother who wanted no more feuds. Nevertheless, no answer or thanks were ever received from Maria or from any of her family. Not long after this, Victoria and Pilar heard that the Oil Refinery Project had been shelved once again due to the continuing financial crisis.

So life went on as normal in the Badajoz pueblo, and like many towns in the Spanish interior, time didn't seem to touch it, or taint it. The attractive Extremeña women get married to their long time boyfriends, have their one or two children, and often reach middle age overweight. The young men are smart and well dressed, rarely change their appearances or hairstyles, and normally don´t grow beards or plaster themselves with tattoos! The older men and pensioners sit down in the shade and watch the world go by equally well dressed, and never wearing shorts, even in high summer! Tractors may have replaced the mules their fathers and grandfathers used, but these men are as tough and gnarled as the land they worked on.

The ailing Donald Breck was given a new lease of life when his great nephew James told him about Pilar and Victoria, and he gazed at the photos of them for a long time before commenting. "Pilar is still attractive and elegant, but the girl is a real good looker, just like her great-grandmother!"

"You still remember it all, don't you uncle?", asked James.

"I do that son, as if it was yesterday". He went quiet as if pondering, then suddenly said, "Well my boy, we have some new material now for you to include in the follow up book, and very important it is too".

"But we still need that *missing piece* uncle. We don't know where that bloody Gibraltar document was hidden sixty six years ago", the boy sounded frustrated.

"Listen son, I know where it is".

"You do?", answered his nephew, much surprised.

"Ever since 2008 when those last files were released I read the statements by the police and special agents who were involved, and I have formed an idea", replied Donald gravely.

"Will you tell me?", asked the younger man.

"Not just at the moment no, but I want you to be the one to find it and keep it safe", replied the old man.

"Can't you tell me anything yet?", he pleaded.

"Yes, but first of all are you still a member of that Steam Preservation Society?", he asked crptically.

"I'm still a member yes, replied James, "I help occasionally at Midsomer Hollow Station when I have time".

"Good, replied the old man, "have you any holidays left this year?"

James had no idea where this conversation was going, but he did know that his great uncle didn't waste words.

"I have two more weeks that I can take when I like, provided I give the office a week or so notice, why uncle?", he asked.

Donald answered him with a further question, "How far have they restored the old railway line".

"About quarter of a mile, as far as I know", remarked James.

The Midsomer Hollow Station building had survived where many others on the old Somerset and Dorset Railway had been demolished, or allowed to fall into decay. A dedicated band of volunteers had dug out the original platform, laid rails, and had steam trains running on the line once more, even if only over a short stretch of track.

This station had regularly won prizes for its marvellously well-kept gardens back in steam's heyday, and had even had its own greenhouse next to the signal box!

"You know that they plan to extend the line all the way to the Eastcompton Tunnel again, and even to Eastcompton itself?", Donald asked the boy.

"Of course, answered James, "but that's going to be a hell of a job, parts of the line are overgrown and some even filled in. Why uncle, have they had permission to extend?".

"I believe so, said the elder, "and what you said is true. Before the line entered the Eastcompton Tunnel there was a very deep cutting, and it has been filled in by tons and tons of builder's rubble and household refuge. It will be a big job digging all that out again, and it will cost a lot of money".

James was still puzzled, but his uncle asked him to get his large scale map of the old S&D trackbed.

"Look here", he said, flattening the map out on the table......

The British weather put paid to any long term work at the moment however, and the rest of August and most of September was wet and windy. Eventually, the work of digging out and extending the old railway track was put back to the next Spring. The more James thought about the theory his uncle had explained to him regarding the missing document, the more he believed in it, and he was impatient to start the search. It seemed incredible that two people had lost their lives on that same,short section of railway track back in 1948, and at least three others had died elsewhere. Arancha had been shot in a quiet lane, the Spanish envoy was murdered in London and the former MI5 chief had been killed in a car crash, also in a Somerset. All five of them had lost their lives in connection with the secret and elusive Spanish/British Agreement.

The two young people kept in touch by e mail and the occasional phone call, and James was delighted when Victoria agreed to come to England again in the Spring, only this time to Somerset.

By the time late May was here, work on digging out and restoring the section of the old S&D line to Eastcompton Tunnel was well under way.

James met Victoria at Bristol Airport , and drove her through the green-lined lanes towards home. "If I ever have to give directions to anyone how to get to and fro from this airport, I don't think I could do it!".

Victoria laughed. The open car window blew the hair in her face, and the air smelt fresh and clean. Occasionally the smell of cows or pigs drifted in, but this was better than the smog of Madrid, she thought.

After about forty minutes driving they reached Stanten, and drove straight to Donald.s house.
The old man had deteriorated during the winter and early spring months, and they found him propped up in bed reading. His housekeeper/cook greeted the couple, and told them lunch was

prepared. "Your uncle has had his already, she said, "you had better go on up before he has his nap".

"You see Victoria, James aid laughing, "we have our siesta here too!"

Victoria could see straight away that although Donald Breck may be in his late eighties and dying, he was still clean, tidy and alert. His eyes sparkled as he kissed Victoria. She could smell a good aftershave on him, but noticed in that fraction of a section that old men don't shave well, probably because their eyesight is failing. It was a ridiculous thing to notice she thought,but small whiskers were on his upper lip just under his nose. She had taken a liking to Mr Breck straight away.

"Hello my dear, at last, he said to the Spanish woman in a clear voice, "I hope you had a good journey. Is your grandmother well?.

When the greetings were completed, the two said that they would leave him to rest, while they ate.

"Yes, you must both be starving, said Donald, "we have things to discuss later!"

"Not before I give you a little gift from Spain", laughed Victoria.

"I will look forward to it!", he replied happily. As he watched the couple leave, he noticed that James took her hand in his own.

After tea, Donald had his maps and diagrams laid out on the bed. "We both want you to be part of this Victoria", he told her. James had already explained to her that his uncle had a hunch, or maybe more than a hunch, where the missing document had been hidden all these years.

Victoria had read "The Bloodstained Document", and remembered that this contract had passed from the Spanish Government to the UK via their envoy, had been stolen by her grandmother's father, been hidden by him, and later found by a paid accomplice of Ian Green of MI5. He had hidden it so well that MI5, the police, and everyone else were at a loss as to where it was. Eventually the danger to the British Governmant passed, but if the document were ever found it could still cause an international incident, or acute embarrassment to Britain at the very least. Rumours of the existence of an agreement handing Gibraltar back to Spain were one thing, but actual physical evidence was another.

"Do you think the document will be preserved, Mr Breck, she asked, "and still legible?.

"Call me Donald please dear" he answered smiling. "Yes, I would think so. They should have made sure that it was kept in some sort of wallet, or pouch".

"Written documents can last for fifty or one hundred years easily, in the right conditions", remarked James.

Donald agreed. "More than that of course, for centuries even. Our one would need to be not bent or creased, and to have been kept in a dark, dry atmosphere".

"Surely you don't mean it to be under all that, *basura*? How do you say.....", asked Victoria.

"Rubbish, helped James, "or in this case, tons and tons of rubbish and rubble".

"Ah yes, *escombros*. But you would never find it, let alone intact".

By way of answer, Donald asked her to look at the railtrack map again, and pointed out two rectanglular shapes. He then showed her a diagram and asked, "Do you know what these are?"

Victoria's face lit up, and she said, "They are *búnkers*". Then, she looked at the description on the diagram. "You call them *peelbokses*?"

"Exactly, said Donald, pillboxes!".

The old man started coughing, and looked tired. "Lie back uncle, said James, "take it easy and I will explain to her".

Donald nodded, and the girl fluffed up his pillow and laid his head down. She thought how light he felt.

James took up the commentary. "This stretch of railway between Midsomer Hollow Station and the Eastcompton Tunnel had two pillboxes, they were erected during World War Two. You know, for protection. Soldiers inside could fire rifles or machine guns through the embrasures".

"*Embrasters*?", she copied.

James didn't smile. "Embrasures, the slits in the walls".

"Tell me more, said Victoria, I like details".

"Well, the two we are looking for, and hope are still there are called Type 24. They are actually hexagon shaped, with a back wall of over 4 metres long. There was a door in this wall, with two embrasures each side. The other five shorter walls were about 2.5 metres long, and they each had one embrasure each. The walls were about 30cm thick".

Victoria was impressed, and turned to Donald. "And you think this *fugitivo* pushed the document into one of those slits, but what gave you the idea?.

"By reading the statements from the time, explained James, "when Ian Green the disgraced MI5 boss was taken from the crashed car, he was still alive. In the ambulance he was questioned by a Detective Harris who was in charge of the whole investigation down here in Somerset".

"And?", asked Victoria, impatient now.

"Green stuttered out that he never quite made it to the pill, or words to that effect", he explained.

"So why didn't the police, or whoever search the *búnkers*?", she asked.

"Because he only said pill, not pillbox, answered James, "they thought he meant a pill, something like a cyanide pill. He was on the run and knew he couldn't get away, he was disgraced and would probably have been executed as a spy or at least imprisoned for life".

"So they thought he tried to kill himself by crashing the car instead", Victoria mused.

Donald lifted himself up and said, "He probably did anyway, but not quite for the reason they thought. In the reports it tells how Green stole the car in the railway station carpark, but after he had been seen loitering around there"

He lay down again, and James said to the girl, "Somehow Green must have guessed that the pillbox was the hiding place, perhaps there was some agreement between him and his accomplice. That is one of the mysteries. We only know that he didn't have the time or opportunity to find the right pillbox. Perhaps that was it, he knew the agreement had been placed in one of them, but not which one. And also as Donald pointed out, this Tanner man left his note in the railway left luggage office, and it mentioned that the document was in a safe place and shockproof. A pillbox is shockproof".

"I think the American Dodd had sussed that out too", remarked Donald, a little breathlessly.

"And now you have the same problem", she smiled at them both.

"Correction Victoria, *we* have the same problem, you are coming with me to search those things as soon as they have been unearthed. That why I am taking my holidays!"

"It will be an honour", she replied with a smile.

"It was his idea, replied James, looking at Donald, "'but knowing him, he probably has an ulterior motive".

"But, he continued, "our job shouldn't be that difficult as we know where the bunkers are, and hopefully we won't have the police or MI5 on our backs!"

"Won't these *búnkers* have collapsed, or be full of water?, asked Victoria.

Donald shook his head, and James said for him, "We are hoping that they will be intact, and Uncle thinks that the embrasures would have been sealed or bricked up. Many of them were by the authorities, maybe for safety, or to stop children being over inquisitive".

The elder Breck was breathing heavily, but managed to say, "It's amazing that hundreds of pill boxes and tank traps were built all over the country ready for the German invasion, but thank God they never had to used".

"We have several *miradores* still standing in Spain, said Victoria, but they are much, much older".

"Yes I know, said James, I stayed in Benalmádena once, and they have a couple of those watchtowers there. They are kept in very good condition".

"And how will we get into this *peelbok*?", she asked.

"Good question, James answered her, "the door will obviously have been sealed up somehow. We just don't know for sure until we see it, but hopefully won't have to ask for outside help".

Victoria went quiet, then asked Donald, "What will you do with the document *if* you find it, and *if* it is in good condition?"

Donald rang the little bell he had on his bedside table, and said evasively ",Let's all have another cup of tea!"

The two young people didn't mind, they were very fond of each other and of Donald, and were looking forward to this *adventure*. Soon though, the couple's lighthearted mood would be tested as storm clouds were gathering.

CHAPTER 29

Alfonso Martin was the lawyer who had worked for the family of Pilar's stepsister in Badajoz, and his professional pride had been hurt when put in his place by Antonio Guillen. Guillen, Pilar's Madrid lawyer had sent Martin proof of Pilar's identity, so he had no option but to drop their action. However, even if the family had to eat crow he would still try to get something out of this, and not only for financial reasons. He wondered why Pilar had been born in England and been adopted by the Pardo family, and was now searching his memory for something he had heard a few years previously. He decided to call on Maria and Manolo, and phoned them for an appointment.

His reception was a bit frosty at first. Martin's fees had been quite high, only for the family to lose the claim on their house, but they soon warmed when he told them that he was investigating Pilar's case again.

Maria told the lawyer all she knew about Pilar's past, and that of her father and uncle, and surmised about the rest.

"Are you aware of anyone she is in contact with in *Inglaterra*?" he asked.

She answered in the negative, and Alfonso could see that he wasn't going to learn much more from the family. He took his leave, and started the forty minute drive back to Badajoz city.

As he drove and watched the signposts go past, Santa Marta, Don Benito etc. he thought, and suddenly it came to him! A few years ago, was it really seven? Spanish newspapers had carried a report about secret files newly released by the British Government after a lapse of sixty years. It was coming back to him now, two Spaniards working for the Russians had stolen a document that in 1948 was dynamite. Apparently the British drew up an agreement with Franco in 1939 to dissuade him from entering the war on the side of the Nazis. His reward would have been joint ownership of the Rock of Gibraltar, followed by Spanish ownership of it after seventy years! "*Coño*, said Martin under his breath, "WW2 ended in 1945, so seventy years from then would have been this year". He resolved to look up the matter as soon as he reached his office.

By evening, Alfonso had gleaned from the web all the known facts of the 1948 spy case, and he had also found out about Donald Breck's book on the affair. As he was also fluent in English, had started to read....

Within a couple of days Martin was ready to act, and his first move was to contact a friend in the local Junta de Extremadura, the region's autonomous government.

Within days, questions were asked in the Madrid Parliament. A member of the Socialist Opposition demanded of the Prime Minister what had been done in light of this information, especially as his government put top priority in reclaiming Gibraltar for Spain. This was a mistake. "If I remember, boomed the PM, "there was a socialist government in power in 2008, so perhaps your questions should be directed to your former Ministers".

"Don't try to dodge the issue Prime Minister, answered his questioner, "you have been in power for several years now, so there must have been information available and not acted on".

The Prime Minister responded with, "Of course there must have been, and the relevant departments will give me an update tomorrow".

Heckling started form the opposition benches, but the PM stood up and remarked acidly, "I know more about this affair than perhaps you give me credit for. There has been no cover up from my ministers, but perhaps there was from your previous government when they found out that the two Spanish spies shot and killed in Britain were fugitive Republicans working for the Soviet Union".

Within days the Press Office had released information to the main newspapers, and a report had been wrangled stating that a lawyer in Extremadura claimed to know the identity of the spy's love child. He would only say that "he had the woman's privacy to respect", but that "she had recently visited Great Britain and almost certainly had knowledge of the whereabouts of a misplaced Gibraltar Agreement". What he didn't state was that the agreement dated back to 1939!

Alfonso Martin was no fool, and he knew that even if the agreement were found legible, too many years had gone by to render it valuable. However, the affair would make a great story, the people will be shouting "Gibraltar is legally ours", and government will have to act. Martin, like his friend in the Junta, was no friend of the current right wing government, and a scandal accusing them of incompetence would do no harm. Of course though, if the press wanted his story, they would have to pay and pay well.

Before Martin could start his *Gibraltar Fever* though, Britain's Ambassador to Spain was called to see their Foreign Minister in Madrid. In a friendly and cordial atmosphere, Nicholas Dewey the Ambassador, was asked unofficially what his government knew about the Gib affair, and if there were any latest developments that he knew of. Dewey made light of the whole affair, stating that of course a book written by D. Breck after the release of secret files had carried the text of the supposed agreement, but this document was long lost or destroyed, and it wouldn't have any credence now anyway.

"Maybe not Nicholas, maybe not, replied the Minister de Asuntos Exteriores, "but will the Spanish people be satisfied with that explanation. You know, there is a lawyer here who is threatening to expose the daughter of this Arancha woman in the book".

The implication was clear, the minister had made a veiled threat to make the whole story public unless, unless what?

"So what do you want from me Minister?" asked Dewey.

"Your cooperation in checking out what this woman knows, he replied smoothly, "we know she went to England last year with her granddaughter to collect her birth certificate from Somerset House".

"Innocent enough", remarked Dewey.

"Of course, replied the Minister, "but the granddaughter is over there again, right now. We would like to know why she is there, and who she is in contact with". He laughed, "Of course, there is no question of espionage any more in this day and age, but a story is about to break here. Imagine the papers, the magazines, the tv shows. They will all want to find this woman and make as much as they can from it. We don't want to be embarrassed by it, and I'm sure your government doesn't either", he continued.

Dewey still thought it was all rubbish, but said, "You had better give me the names of this woman and her granddaughter then Minister".

Just as he was speaking, a plains clothes Guardia Civil officer was ringing the bell of Pilar's apartment in another part of the city.

CHAPTER 30

The next morning Victoria received a Whatsapp from her grandmother telling her about the police visit, and the paper stories. "They knew you were in England, and wanted to know exactly where, who you were with and what you were doing. Had to tell them, you know what GC can be like, you had better phone me".

When she told James he was surprised, but not particulary worried. "Someone has caught hold of the story and wants to make some money out of it, that's all, he remarked, "it just makes our search more difficult if the media is on to us".

Pilar confirmed that she had to answer most of the questions, including admitting that she was the daughter of Juan Pardo and Arancha. She told the detective that she knew nothing about an agreement, apart from what Victoria had read about in the book and related to her. As to why her granddaughter was in England, she replied that she and James Breck, a relation of the book's author were now close friends. They had met last year in London, and they were now in Somerset where they would presumably visit the 1948 spy locations, she related.

"Good, said James to Victoria, very good. Especially the bit about us being good friends!" and kissed her.

The two pondered on whether they should tell Donald about these new developments, and finally decided that they must.

Donald took the news philosophically, and then with his usual humour and quick brain said, "If they want a story, by God we'll give them one". Slapping his leg lightly under the bedclothes, he called the two young people nearer.

"They will have the media here now alright, he said, enjoying himself, "so when the time is right we will disclose where the agreement is hidden, and they can film us recovering it live!"

James and Victoria were initially stunned, but then saw that Donald was serious and had a plan!

"So, uncle, said James guessing what the old man had in store, "presumably we find the document first, then stage a *second finding*?

"Exactly my boy", replied Donald, not looking tired at all.

"And how will the second document differ from the real one?" he asked, "Provided we find it".

"God willing, you leave that to me, he answered, "until I need your help that is", he grinned.

Victoria caught James'eye however, and gently shook her head.

"You have a rest uncle, said James, "and we will discuss it again later".

When they got downstairs the housekeeper had gone out shopping.

"How can we do what he said?, asked Victoria, "the document doesn't belong to us, and everyone will know now where it is. That isn't going to help your book, is it?"

James thought before replying. "You are right of course, if the public and media are told about the search, then we shall have no rights to whatever we may find inside that pillbox. *If* we find anything that is", he added.

"It's common knowledge that we are here, so it won't be long before, what is it you say... *two and two are four*?, asked the girl.

"Something like that yes, replied James absent mindedly, "so as we have little choice why not publicise everything, and make as much as we can from it?".

"You are *serious*?", asked Victoria.

"Yes, listen, he continued, "we can use this to our advantage. In exchange for our information and intentions, the tv stations or whoever, can pay for the site to be cleared. The Railway Preservation Society will get part of their work done for them for free. They can also arrange and pay for the pillbox to be opened up. I must admit that part has been worrying me".

Victoria listened intently, then replied, "And if the document is found in there?"

"Then I'm afraid we will have to give it up. Presumably it will be the property of the British government, although I shall insist that we get to look at it first, and demand first publishing rights if any are granted".

"And you will tell Donald?, asked Victoria.

"If I think he can stand it yes... when the time is right".

James and Donald had a phone call the next day from an official of the civil service, who arranged to come and meet them the following morning. The whole business was discussed mainly with James, as the civil servant told him that the authorities seemed uneasy at having a Spanish subject present due to the circumstances! Although the two of them agreed this was absurd, they spoke frankly and both put forward their various interests and priorities.

"There can be no question of making a show out of this with live tv coverage Mr Breck, said John Henshaw, the official, "you must understand that".

"Of course, replied James, and I don't desire it. Unfortunately though we are being followed now by both the British and Spanish media and God knows who else, and they will be expecting answers. I only wanted to try to find this document to allow me to finish writing my uncle's book".

The meeting broke up amiably, and Henshaw told Breck that he would be contacted again shortly.

The interested government department must have put some importance to the matter, as Henshaw returned the next day. Victoria was welcome to listen in this time.

"What we have decided Mr Breck, is that clearage of the rail track site will proceed with all haste, then when the pillbox in question is exposed, the area will be cordoned off. Workmen will attempt to open the bunker, and the three of us together will examine its interior".

"But won't that attract attention?", asked Victoria.

Henshaw smiled at her and said, "No Miss, the police will be patrolling a large area all around the site, but discreetly, and at night".

"And if we find anything inside?, asked James.

"If we find the document that you think is there, or any other item that is government property, then we will read it together. I will then decide whether or not it is confidential, and the two of you will be sworn to secrecy under threat of prosecution under the Official Secrets Act".

It all sounded rather dangerous to the girl, and James had to smile when Henshaw finished by asking, "Is that fair?"

The two said yes it was, "But what about the media?", asked James.

"Ah, replied John, "this is the clever bit. A day or two later we can stage another, fake opening, and we will allow one or two people to be there to film. Of course, if the document is legible and compromising, then we may have to substitute it".

"Not too far from Donald's original idea then", commented James.

"Pardon?", asked Henshaw.

"Oh nothing, just thinking aloud!", replied James.

"I am talking about how we present any find to the media of course. What will happen at government level doesn't concern us", replied Henshaw.

"Of course", agreed Breck, tongue in mouth.

The village of Stanten-on-the-Fosse hadn't changed or grown much over the years. Some council estates had gone up during the early fifties and been demolished again, and all of its four shops had now disappeared, including the village post office. The colliery situated between Stanten and Eastcompton had long been closed and its slagheap levelled out, so that strangers were surprised to hear that there ever was a flourishing coal mining industry in Somerset at all.

The no-through road where the 1948 shooting took place was now nothing more than a muddy track, and a burnt-out and abandoned car blocked its entrance. James and Victoria had their jeans and wellington boots on, and a light rain started to fall as they edged their way past the vehicle. The hedges on both sides had been left to grow wild, and in places they met in the middle of the lane, making it difficult and pointless to push through them. The two climbed over a gate instead, and continued walking down the fields until they came to the site of old Granny Wilson's cottage. Try as they might though, they could find no trace of it, not even a single stone.

Work was progressing well in clearing the old railway cutting of its thousands of tons of overspill, and except for one or two trusted people, the volunteers of the Railway Preservation Society were kept ignorant of what was being planned. Their participation in the project was kept to a minimum, and it was put around that a plant company had been hired for this heavy work, and that they wanted non-employees kept away for safety reasons.

The actual railtrack bed was now exposed, by way of digging a tunnel-like pathway all the way up to where the pillbox was reckoned to be. Apart from it being narrower, the cutting was beginning to look like it once was, but care had to be taken to dump the debris behind the machines as they dug into it. There were now high mountains on either side of the trackbed, and care had to be taken by the contractors to prevent slippage. The pillbox would have been situated close to the railway line, and on the east or righthand side looking towards Norton Hollow. Once the approximate pillbox site was reached, a slope was formed about 20 metres in front of it so that the diggers could climb up and start clearing away from the top and at right angles, until the structure was unearthed.

At last the digger struck concrete, and from then on the work was carried out slowly and carefully until the pillbox and a safe portion of earth around it was dug out. Work stopped, and the police sergeant nearby phoned his station where the news was passed on to Henshaw and Breck, who were waiting at home. They, Victoria and a couple of burly constables were led along the eerie path cut into the spoil heap, and James wondered if the rest of the work was now going to be made easier or more difficult for the volunteers, for it was they who would eventually have to widen it to its full width.

The box looked in good condition as the party arrived, and the embrasures seemed to be blocked up. "That's good, thought James, "it could mean the box is empty. Depends what had happened to it beforehand though".

The thick door had also been sealed up with cement, so one of the PC's went to work on it with a heavy hammer and mason's chisel. When the door was opened, the sergeant told the other constable to bring up the portable generator and lights that he had carried to the site. The strong lights were pushed through the now open doorway on the end of a pole, and a strong smell of rotting vegetation and decay made Victoria shudder and feel sick.

"After you?", Henshaw asked James.

The other nodded, and pushed his head inside. All the floor of the bunker was covered in what looked like about 10cm of rubble, but it was dry. Henshaw followed James inside, and a constable handed them a metal rake. They moved to the side where the blocked up embrasures faced the railway line, and started their search there.

An A4 sized leather pouch was soon turned up, looking in a remarkably good condition, and laying flat amongst the dust and rubble. An emblem was apparent on the pouch. James touched the pouch carefully with the rake, and was pleased to see that it didn't fall apart or disintegrate! Both men had thin gloves on, and James bent down and picked the pouch up. The emblem on the pouch was that of Nationalist Spain. "They aren't allowed to display that anymore!", commented Henshaw.

Nervous fingers pulled out the leather closure flap, and they were surprised that no lock of any type was present. A single sheet of paper was inside, dry, but with its writing very faint. With the sheet still half inside its pouch, the two men moved it closer to the light, and read.....

They both looked stunned, then surprised and puzzled, then they both laughed at the same time.

"It's been changed! cried James, "But by whom?"

"Nothing in this to compromise us", said Henshaw, obviously relieved.

"A lot of money for nothing eh?", remarked James.

Henshaw laughed and said, "My department will send you their bill as soon as your book has made you its fortune!".

The door of the bunker was pushed back into place, and plans were laid for its *second opening* tomorrow. Victoria was told that a reporter from a Spanish tv channel would be present, along with other invited pressmen and media. They wouldn't get what they were hoping for, but it was still a good story, and this was still a remarkable find.

"But who could have changed the wording in the agreement James?", she asked on their way home.

"Well, I've been thinking that it could only have been either Ian Green, or that Gerald Tanner who found it here in the railway tunnel".

"But that doesn't make sense does it James? Victoria asked, "One of those men got killed, and the other tried to kill himself... for something they knew was useless? And they wouldn't have had the time or facility to tamper with a document anyway".

"In that case, the only other possibility was that Juan Pardo tampered with the document himself. Maybe your relation wasn't so bad after all Victoria, he laughed, "we have some more research to do and this time no one will find the outcome unless they buy the book!"

"But I have to be going back to Madrid soon", cried Victoria.

"When?", asked James, kissing her.

"Soon!"

EPILOGUE

James finished his book a year later, but although Donald Breck didn't live quite long enough to see it published, he did know what new content it contained. In fact, he had helped his great nephew with the research into unravelling the mystery as much as he could, and the two were pretty sure that what they had documented was as near as damn it to the truth. Neither did Donald ever get to meet Pilar in person, although he died happy in the knowledge that her granddaughter and James were engaged to be married some time in the future.

The second edition of "The Bloodstained Document" sold well, both as an e book and as a paperback, and it stimulated renewed controversy in Britain, Spain and Gibraltar, where it was released with lavish publicity.

Juan Pardo was indeed responsible for tampering with the Gibraltar agreement. It will never be fully known why he did it, but Breck made the following assumptions:

1. That Pardo read the document after he had killed and robbed it from the Spanish envoy, and either didn't like what it contained ie that the hated Franco regime would get Gibraltar back, or that he thought the document was a waste of time and would never be successful. Maybe he wrongly thought that his Russian masters would be displeased with him, and he could have even possibly been afraid that they were planning to liquidate him after the job was done.

2. He had had a change of heart about the Russians, and became disillusioned with their tactics. About the way they had performed in the Civil War, and maybe about the way they had tempted him with the release of his brother from Siberia.

It's likely that Pardo decided to deceive the Russians and settle for the 1000 pounds he had robbed from the Duke of Avila, rather than continue in their pay. Speculation is that he and Arancha planned to fly to Buenos Aries together, but he had to lay low for a couple of days and find somewhere to hide the document. He would probably have given his Russian contacts the coded whereabouts of the agreement, but only after he and his lover had left England. Possibly he only gave Arancha vague details as a precaution.

What does seem a coincidence, is that Downbury was involved in both the adoption process of Arancha's child, and the visits of both the real and fake Spanish envoys. These involvements were innocent enough though, and probably based on connections of faith and friendship.

The retrieved, and tampered with agreement between the British Government and the Official Government of Spain which was drawn up in 1940, was placed in Donald Breck's coffin, and buried with him in Stanten's cementery.

It ran more as a declaration than an official agreement, but possibly gives some idea of Pardo's thinking.

The changed wording of the agreement in full was as follows:

"His Majesty's Government hereby give notice that they formally recognise the Nationalist Government of Spain, and accept General Francisco Franco Bahamonde as its leader.

Furthermore, His Majesty's Government would like to stress that they implicitly kept a neutral stance during Spain's recent three years of civil war.

Now, the roles are reversed as Britain finds itself in a state of war against Nazi Germany and her Axis partners, and it will be hoped that Spain will maintain a neutral position while these hostilities last.

Britain fully understands Spain's current difficult position, and appreciates its past ties with both Nazi Germany and Italy, but it must do everything in its power to protect itself, its Commonwealth, and its overseas interests, especially those in the Mediterranean.

With this in mind, His Majesty's Government feel that the Rock of Gibraltar, together with its town, waters and possessions must be prevented from falling into enemy hands at all costs. In exchange for Spain's neutrality in the war, Britain, at the end of hostilities, will endeavour to negotiate with Soviet Russia for the return of all of Spain's gold reserves, which at this present time are still deposited in the Soviet Union".

"What about our Spanish gold then?, asked Victoria saucily.

"Well, you measure my finger for size, replied James, "and I will measure yours!"

THE END

14864008R00071

Printed in Great Britain
by Amazon.co.uk, Ltd.,
Marston Gate.